Blackberry Jam

Every man writes his own moral code. Some of us do it in crayon. Hotdog's accident was forcing me to be a much better friend than is typically required of me, and I was already furious. The smell of hospital disinfectant wasn't quite strong enough to mask the stench of despair and the fluorescent lights made even the healthy visitors look sallow and sickly. It occurred to me how perverse and morbid it is to bring babies into the world in the same hellhole everyone else leaves it. I swallowed this thought. This was no time for an existential crisis. I'd save that for the bus trip home. I approached the counter and became another thing for the clearly overworked and harried nurse (Ham and Cheese) to deal with. She had angry eyebrows but sad eyes. In an effort to brighten her day, I decided to be extremely polite and friendly.

"Hello. I'm looking for my friend." I found myself whispering. Hospital disinfectant and church frankincense somehow demand sombre whispers. Something in me felt constrained and rebelled against this. I wasn't sick. I tried again in a healthier tone.

"Hi. I'm looking for my mate. His legs are broken. His na-"

"I know the one" The nurse interrupted in a no nonsense, professional tone.

"Third floor. Ward six."

I thanked her very politely, but my efforts didn't seem to have brightened her day. I made my way to Hotdog's ward. The air was

1

stagnant and warm. Soupy. I was convinced I was inhaling River Blindness and The Black Death. Why don't hospital windows open? I kept my eyes front and centre, observing as little as possible. The worst thing about having to run this gauntlet of tragedy was how hard-done-by I was feeling. And seriously, why the hell don't hospital windows open? I took off my jacket before I even got to Hotdog's room.

Hotdog was on a ward with actual grown-ups. Three and a half decades experience being children qualifies us as adults apparently. His roommates were a middle-aged man (Tuna Mayo) with a bandage over his left eye concealing an unknown affliction, and an old man (Blackberry Jam) hooked up to loads of machines, who was clearly on his death bed. The only thing that saved me from gaping like an idiot was not being able to decide which one to ogle at. My friend was in the corner bed by the window. Hotdog has the looks of a handsome film star, but while he's giving an Oscar worthy performance and managing to somehow act his way out of being sexy. He looked even more miserable than usual propped up in the bed. As I got closer, I saw a priest (Avocado Toast) behind the partially pulled curtain, sitting with him. I was about to turn and leg it when Holy Guacamole spotted me. I wasn't getting out of this. Way overcompensating for my hesitation, I strutted over to them like a bloody Bee Gee.

"Look at the fucking state of you." I said to Hotdog. The last thing you should indulge sick people with is sympathy. It lends credence to their concerns. If everyone's still being horrible to you, things can't be that serious. Using Hotdog as a human shield, I hung my jacket over the back of the chair on the other side of the bed from the priest while fighting the urge to think up a dozen tragic back stories for people who'd sat there before me.

"I'll leave you to talk with your friend. I'll see you tomorrow

2

In HindSpite

By T. Bolger

For my parents. I tried to keep the cursing to the bare minimum, but unfortunately, that's still fucking loads.

It took a hell of a lot of pep talks from a hell of a lot of people to get all these words on all these pages.

You know who you are. And I do too.

please God." Holy Guacamole said while giving me a filthy, Catholic look.

"Yes Father. Thanks very much for stopping by." said Hotdog.

The priest left in a huff. As soon as he was out of earshot, Hotdog turned on me and hissed, "You're not supposed to curse in front of a priest dickhead!"

"He's a grown man. Fuck him." I hiss back. "If he doesn't like it, he can go right ahead and forgive me. Was he giving you your last rites, or what?"

"You really shouldn't take the piss. Faith is a great source of comfort and joy in people's lives." Hotdog says with a sincerity that'd turn your stomach.

"Yeah. You're a real poster boy for that, you morose fucker. Now, before you start whinging, Three Things."

Generally, Hotdog is as miserable as I am, but he's a lot more vocal about it. You have to be very careful not to ask him how he is because he'll bloody tell you. I instated The Three Good Things Policy with him ages ago. Basically, I promised to listen to him whinging whenever he wanted with a bare minimum of sarcastic interruptions, but he'd have to list Three Good Things first. I thought it would cheer him up to have to think about good stuff. Honestly, it hasn't done him that much good, but he has come up with some proper whimsical short lists.

"- A puppy leaping his way through fields of barley so he can see where he's going

- The tingling, staticky feeling of the screen when you turn on our ancient tellies

- The *Boing* noise when you flick one of those door stopper spring things."

"Good ones." I admit.

"I've been here all day." He whinges.

3

"OK, let's have a look at you. You must be roasting under those blankets."

Before he could protest, I pulled away his sheet like a magician pulling a tablecloth from under a set of dishes to reveal one of those short hospital dress things and two legs in casts from his knees to his toes covered in graffiti and language that would make even an Australian's eyes water.

"Jesus! How are you already covered in that filth?"

"I don't know. I woke up from the operation looking like a mobile pub toilet wall."

"Well, you're not *that* mobile, are you? I see why you were covered up in front of the priest."

"Don't get me started." he sighs.

"What the fuck happened?"

"It's a bit embarrassing actually."

"I'm sure it is pal. There's wiser eating grass." I did feel sorry for him, but I feel I hid it well.

"Me and the new fella at work were coming back from helping a customer carry her shopping to the car park when it came up that he'd never seen *Cool Runnings,* so I was recreating key scenes for him." Hotdog and I own two videotapes. One of them is *Cool Runnings*

Cool Runnings

Cool Runnings is a 1993 comedy starring John Candy about three Jamaican runners and their comic relief friend who decide to become bobsledders and compete in the winter Olympics. It's brilliant!

"I was pushing a bunch of trolleys up the hill doing the 'Feel the rhythm, feel the ride' bit and I slipped."

"Wait! You ran yourself over? Like Brian fucking Harvey?"

"Yeah." he whispers.

4

Brian Harvey

Brian Harvey was the lead singer of 90s boyband *East 17*. They were brilliant! In 2005, after eating three tuna mayo jacket potatoes, he got out of his car without putting on the handbrake and it rolled over him. This is widely considered to be one of the most idiotic accidents to ever have occurred.

"This new fella at work? Is he handsome?" I ask.

"What? Why? I don't know." Hotdog splutters. I nearly said something then but thought better of it.

"Have you heard from work?" I asked instead.

"Yeah, they sent me grapes and 7Up." There were five unopened bottles of 7Up and a mountain of grapes on his bedside locker.

"They brought you all of that?"

"No. Every visitor I've had brought the same thing."

"Do you like 7Up and grapes?"

"Despise them. They remind me of being sick as a kid." I picked up my backpack and gave him a guilty look.

"You better be joking." He sighs.

"Fear not. You're in for a treat kid. I have brought you ..." I paused for effect and to wrestle with the zip. This was clearly the closest to excitement Hotdog had come all day. He leant forward until he winced.

"I have brought you. Are you ready?"

"Don't toy with me man. I'm on the edge here." He warns.

"OK. I have brought you" I whipped each thing out as I named it.

"All the clean underpants in your top drawer. You've only got four pairs. So, you know. Get well soon."

"OK."

5

"A family pack of Capri Sun."

"Yes!"

"Annnnddd a box of Milk Tray with the coffee ones pre-binned."

"Yes!"

"Annnndd my old Gameboy with original Super Mario before graphics got fancy."

"YES!"

"Annnndd my ex's old, pink iPod shuffle that I found in a drawer."

"Thank God!"

"I'll warn you now. Having this music on shuffle is like playing limbo with an electric fence. In the dark. In 1986."

"As long as it's loud. You have no idea what I've witnessed here today."

"What happened?"

"They're freaks." he whispers.

"Himself with the eye?" I nod over to Tuna Mayo.

"No. He just keeps spilling drinks everywhere. It's the old man and his wife."

"Mate! That man's dying." I scold.

"No, you don't get it." He whispers.

Just then, a border-line fossilised woman (Blackberry Jam), shrunken like a slice of cucumber left in the sun, entered the room and hobbled her way over to the ancient man. She had a blue rinse and a heavy duffle coat buttoned up to her neck despite the soupiness (soupiness is definitely the right word) of the hospital. Her coat had those toggle buttons and everything. There's something about toggle buttons that breaks my heart. You only see them on the oldest people or the youngest kids. I have a crystal-clear memory of my mother doing mine up for me when I was really young, and my fingers weren't nimble enough to do it for myself. The old woman sat down beside her husband and took his old, shrivelled hand in her own like she must have done ten thousand times before. It was as sweet as it was tragic. Old people have always made me feel sad.

"You're looking much better now, my dear" she shouted directly in his face. I hadn't seen him earlier, but if that old man had looked any worse, he'd have been dead. It struck me then that lying to your loved ones can be a great kindness. I couldn't hear his whispered response, but I suddenly had a lump in my throat.

Having a Lump in Your Throat
A male bravado way of saying I was close to tears. I'll try to keep these cop outs to a minimum, but you'll forgive me the occasional one.

"Man, I'm feeling an honest to God feeling here." I admitted to Hotdog.

"Just. You. Wait. He's deaf as a post, so she has to shout at him."

"I brought in the pictures of our honeymoon for you to look at, dear heart. You took me to Paris. I'd always dreamed of going to Paris. You made my dream come true. You kissed me under the Eiffel Tower, and said you'd still love me long after that tower rusted and fell over. Well, it's still standing, so you'll have to put up with me for a long while yet." She bellowed.

She was going to be alone soon. Being alone all the time takes practice. It's a young man's game. At this point, I felt a bit sick.

"Christ!" Hotdog said disgustedly.

"You actually are a sociopath." I chided.

"Wait for it." he said.

"Then you took me to the red-light district, and we picked up

7

that floozy. You just watched. We were your ladies of the night. I still remember. You were as hard as a diamond in a blizzard." She roared.

"Oh God!" I say.

"I've had this since this morning." whispered Hotdog. "They're hedonistic, sexual deviants. She's in here shouting filth at that old man all day."

"I brought you some blackberry jam." She shouted, "It's not as good as mine though. Remember, years ago, if you wanted jam from the shop, you had to bring your own jar, and they'd fill it up for you with a ladle. Remember the signs, 'No Jar, No Jam'. We always made our own though. Every August, we'd bramble for blackberries through the back fields. We'd eat nearly as many as we'd bring home. Then, I'd make the jam. The summers back then seemed to go on forever."

"I think we're on safer ground now." I said.

"Wait." he said holding up a finger, "I give it about four seconds."

"You'd spread it all over me and lap it up like a kitten with a saucer of cream. You'd call me your blackberry tart."

"Mate! Talk to me quick." Hotdog pleaded.

"So, em, what's the story with the guy with the eye?" I asked quietly enough that the man couldn't hear. Unless his hearing had somehow improved to make up for his reduced vision. I'm not entirely sure how that works.

"Apart from *Tales from The Playboy Nursing Home*, inventing biographies for him has been my only distraction all day. He started off as a pirate, but that was a bit predictable. Then he was a Formula One driver who shot himself with a champagne cork while celebrating. Now, he's a disgraced soldier the government are testing a robotic eye on to make him a super soldier."

8

I didn't say, but I thought that was a bit predictable too.

"So, are you gonna make a claim or what?" I asked.

"Directly. Have I been injured in the workplace? Was it not my fault? We're getting jet skis out of this."

"Not your fault? You were impersonating a Jamaican bobsledder in the car park."

"Not on camera, I wasn't. I'm basically Robin Hood." *Robin Hood: Prince of Thieves* is the second video we own.

Robin Hood: Prince of Thieves

Robin Hood, Prince of Thieves is a 1991 action film starring Kevin Costner, Alan Rickman, Morgan Freeman, Mary Elizabeth Mastrantonio and Christian Slater. It's brilliant! The soundtrack features the Bryan Adams song *Everything I Do, I Do It for You* which was No. 1 for sixteen weeks. Everyone got a bit fed up of it during the seventeenth week. Philistines!

We're constantly justifying things by claiming to basically be Robin Hood. This is actually a pretty good example.

"Stealing jet skis from the rich and giving them to the poor?" I ask.

"Exactly. They'll be singing rebel songs about me for a thousand years. It's a supermarket chain, a faceless corporation. I've been mangled in the cogs of their cold, industrial machine as it rolled over me, the little guy." Hotdog once read the back cover of a book on Marxism before putting it under one of the legs of the kitchen table to stop it wobbling.

"So, you're basically a working-class hero, sticking it to the man? Who are you thinking to play you in the film adaptation?"

"I feel the quiet dignity of Tom Hanks could do the role justice." he manages to say with a straight face.

"You know you could get in serious trouble if you get caught?" I said.

"Listen, I've been working in that bloody supermarket for years. It'd be illegal for them to pay us one penny less than they do. They're bigger crooks than The Sheriff of Nottingham."

"To be fair, I went shopping earlier and both 7Up and grapes are on special offer."

"Why am I not surprised? Join the revolution man."

I'm acting unsure, but only because it's hard to be a loose cannon without a voice of reason to play off of. I'm utterly convinced. This is how I like Hotdog best. He does whinge, but there's a wild touch of madness in him too.

"Wait!" I panic, "I'm not going to have to nurse you back to health, am I?"

"No. My parents have invited me home until I'm back on my feet."

"That's very Christian of them. Giving you a sponge bath really wasn't on the cards pal."

"Yeah." He agreed.

"Much better your mother does it."

"I did not think of that." The look of realisation on his face is just turning into panic as the old lady shouts.

"Remember that time during the Blackpool beach gala? After it got dark? You took me behind the spotlights. They couldn't see us. But we could see them. We could see them."

She'd clearly gotten the old man all hot and bothered. He'd gone red in the face. I couldn't hear his reply.

"I'm going to listen to this iPod until my ears bleed." sighed Hotdog.

"That might happen pretty quick." I warned.

"As long as it's not an erotic audiobook narrated by my own

grandmother, I'll absolutely take my chances."

The old man started gasping and the machines began flashing and beeping like a pinball machine. I subtly reached behind me for my coat.

"Well, you seem to be on the mend," I said, "but you need your rest. I guess I should leave you to ge-"

"Don't you fucking dare!" Hotdog snarled at me.

I sighed and slumped back in the chair. Doctors and nurses rushed in and crowded around the old man's bed, while his wife stood aside looking on, wringing her tiny, ancient hands. Then, he just wasn't there anymore. Despite having consistently been there for the best part of a century, he suddenly just wasn't there anymore. They wheeled the bed out of the room. The old woman watched them go. Then she turned to us, two boys on a men's ward, witnessing her grief, looking guilty like children caught with our hands in the biscuit tin, taking something that wasn't offered. She spoke to us, and it was the first time I'd heard her speak without shouting. It was deafening.

"The last thing he says to me was 'Don't you be visiting me grave. I won't be there. You just sing in the shower. I'll be watching you.'" She smiled the saddest smile I've ever seen.

"We've been married for sixty-six years. Never been apart. It sounds like such a long time. We started courting when we were sixteen. But I blinked, and I was thirty. Then I blinked again, and I was fifty. Just look at me now. You youngsters wait so long to start a life now. You think you know something we didn't. You have no idea. There's so little time. I hope you're not wasting it."

She turned and slowly walked out. When she'd gone, I considered saying something flippant to defuse the moment, but she deserved better. No wonder that nurse on was furious. This place was fucking awful. I grabbed my coat and bag and stood up.

11

"Are you crying?" Hotdog accused.

"No. I've got allergies."

"What are you allergic to?"

"My fucking emotions." I spat back.

"It's OK. He's gone to a better place."

"Fuck off! I'll see you when you get out of this hellhole."

Without waiting for a response, I turned and walked out as quickly as was socially acceptable, cursing Hotdog's clumsiness and resolving to make some major life changes. Blackberry jam. Sixty-six years and he still loved blackberry jam.

The Flat

That was two weeks ago. I've taken that old man's death pretty hard. There's been this gnawing in my stomach ever since.

Atheism

There's loads of different types of atheist you can be, but a Catholic atheist is by far the worst. You lose all the walking on water, living forever on a cloud, water into wine, magic bits, but you keep all the guilt and shame stuff.

Feelings are supposed to be nebulous concepts without substance, but they can burn a hole in you from the inside. I've been stuck in a state of crippling urgency for two weeks looking at the wall, doing absolutely nothing, manically thinking about how not to waste my time.

However, I do feel a man should be able to control his emotions. I strictly confine my weeping to the shower. I'm going through enough water to comfortably support a couple of dolphins. Or a very small whale. Between all the water and power used to heat it, my misery is a borderline environmental disaster, but it's important to stay positive. Personal improvement is a big part of that. You should set yourself realistic goals and strive to accomplish them. Set deadlines. I'm aiming to make my misery carbon neutral by 2025. In a rare burst of proactivity the other day, I picked up a bottle of that No More Tears shampoo. As an anti-depressant, it's worse than useless, plus my dandruff has come back.

This morning starts exactly the same as so many before it, in that it doesn't. Everything always seems more impossible in the morning time, so I usually skip it. After a while, I can crawl my way into a semblance of optimism through sheer force of will, but I generally need to work my way up to this. I wake up with the taste of pesto in my mouth and look at the ancient alarm clock beside the bed and sigh. It's the crack of 12:02. I wait until 12:05 to get up. If I miss that sixty second window, I'll be stuck here until 12:10. I stumble into flip flops and stagger to the bathroom. I urinate with 99.6% accuracy. Not bad, but I never go into the bathroom barefoot. I wash my hands and catch a glimpse of myself in the mirror. This isn't something I need to do often. My "look" is so low maintenance that I really only need to check my reflection if I've been eating spaghetti. Old English Sheepdog Chic. I go back to the bedroom and do five hundred sit ups, one hundred push ups and fifty pull ups. This is the one part of my day that's non-negotiable.

I stroll into the living room/kitchen and behold my tiny kingdom. Everyone's been to a flat like this. It's your scruffy, train wreck friend's place that you see once a year. You're too old for this shit, and he really needs to sort himself out (and maybe get a tetanus shot). He's your day pass to revisit the directionless carnage of your youth. You always appreciate your real life more when you get back to it after one of these visits. Turns out, I'm that scruffy train wreck friend. I've lived here for six months. I've been home alone for two weeks now ever since Hotdog got "crushed between the cogs of the capitalist machine". He's staying with his parents while he recuperates. His absence has allowed me to become incredibly anti-social in an amazingly short amount of time. I've even been trying to avoid myself. Trying to avoid myself as a mental exercise is proving to be an exercise in making myself mental. I keep coming up with "clever" quips like this and finding myself tedious for the effort.

I survey my domain. It takes a certain kind of misfit to live in a place like this. 80s lino and 70s wallpaper with those geometric patterns. Artefacts from at least half a dozen previous lives lived here litter the place. They all must have left in a hurry and Hotdog is too much of a hoarder to let me throw anything away.

There's a floor to ceiling bookcase between mine and Hotdog's bedroom doors holding a collection of highbrow English classics and a mishmash of books covering too many tastes, hobbies and interests for one person with two lifetimes and three personalities. We have a drinks cabinet full of obscure but empty bottles you've never heard of from around the world. We've got two tellies from the 80s, one sitting on top of the other. One of them has a broken screen and the other one doesn't have sound but together they just about get the job done. They'd be a good metaphor for me and Hotdog were we to actually get any jobs done. There's a video player to play our film collection. Having an electrical appliance just to watch a John Candy film occasionally does feel a bit ridiculous. We've got a surfboard, an easel, a telescope, a banjo, a saddle, a typewriter, a unicycle and two sewing machines. There's shelves rammed with trophies and cups for half a dozen sports with dates ranging over forty years. No one person is this interesting. No two plates, spoons or cups match. The kitchen has two cookers and an aga that looks like it's from the Industrial Revolution. We have six tin openers.

Our bathroom sink is from a hairdresser's and has that neck dip bit for washing hair. The water pressure is set to pissing racehorse so wetting your crotch while washing your hands is a constant hazard. I own seven towels despite never having bought a towel in my life. I suspect our landlord (Butter Balls) murdered all our predecessors and buried them in the backyard but never bothered getting rid of their stuff.

Cabin fever can set in fast in a place like this. I wouldn't quite say I'm having a nervous breakdown. I might concede that I'm nervous about having a breakdown. Not losing my mind, but briefly and often misplacing it. It's shit quips like this that I'm talking about. I'm fucking intolerable. I've been writing sad haiku like:

I make bitter honey like a depressed bumble bee
I do sad karate like a sad Bruce Lee

This isn't even a haiku. I have no idea what a haiku is, but you get the idea. That's the last time I'll mention poetry, I swear. Anyway, this dandruff is getting to be like a blizzard filter for my vision, so it looks like today is gonna be a Trousers Day. Going outside really shouldn't be an occasion, but I take an hour to psych myself up to putting my shoes on. I often try to motivate myself by thinking of great human accomplishments. If Stephen Hawking can have an affair behind his wife's back despite being entombed in his own body, I can run an errand.

I get to the supermarket and pick up just enough stuff so it doesn't look like I'm having a dry scalp emergency, and I head to the checkouts. It's a disaster. The line of shy losers queuing for the checkout girl with three chins but only one eyebrow (Pork Belly) is unfeasibly long, but it's a straight shot to the intimidatingly pretty girl's (Dijon Turkey) till. I consider doing a lap of honour around the frozen section, but she makes eye contact and there's no escape. I put the max strength dandruff shampoo on the conveyor belt, treadmill thing. I catch Dijon appraising both my head *and* my shoulders. She's looking at me like I'm buying panda poison and granny porn.

16

Resting Bitch Face

This is a relatively new term kids use as a disclaimer for walking about with a facial expression like a rabid Rottweiler. I'm really not sure when being a horrible bastard became a medical condition.

There was nothing "resting" about this bitch's face though. Her malice is so daunting that instead of saying cheers or thanks very much, I get flustered and say, "Cheers very much." I power skulk home and lock the door behind me. I might never leave the flat again. Honestly, if you go outside, anything could happen. I'm whinging. Fuck! I don't think my default mode is quite this miserable, but my heart was left to pickle in camel piss and then two weeks ago, I saw a man die.

There are some idiots who'd say that death is a powerful aphrodisiac, but I've not been feeling at all sexy. Sixty-six years of filth. I've got a pretty wild imagination but even on our best day, I never could have pictured The Pesto Chick screaming sweet nothings into my face after sixty-six years. After a year and a half, we were only having sex on special occasions. I'd considered trying to celebrate Diwali and Chinese New Year. She went cold on me faster than a slice of toast. It was so intense at the beginning. After three weeks, she'd suggested I move into her place. I couldn't believe it. She said it just made sense to help her pay her mortgage instead of me just paying rent where I was, and we were spending most nights together anyway. She was always so practical. I wasn't really listening. I didn't care. I would have gone anywhere with her.

- I'd have lived with her in an explosives shed
- Or a haunted tree house

She started going on about rent and bills but to be honest, it all went over my head.

17

- Or a leaky submarine
- Or a genie's bottle
- Or an abandoned metro station

She rationed out household chores.

- Or a storage room for lost parcels where mysterious packages randomly fall from a chute in the ceiling
- Or an underwater cave lit by bio luminous algae

I would have gone anywhere with her. I swallow this thought. Sorry about that. I get those from time to time.

I unpack the shopping and open the new cereal box. I pour Rice Krispies into a fishbowl that'd been left by a previous tenant. All the people bowls are dirty, and it will take months for erosion to clean them. As the mutilated bits of rice tumble into the bowl, I'm struck by an image of sands falling through an hourglass. In my mind, something crackles, snaps and then pops. *There's so little time. I hope you're not wasting it.* I'd had Rice Krispies yesterday and the day before. Suddenly, and all of my thoughts are sudden just now, jumping out at me like an old flasher from behind a bush wearing nothing but a trench coat, I can't really account for a whole lot of anything. I'm thirty-five years old and all I can vouch for of the last six months is a handful of more embarrassing than memorable incidents. Personal humiliations of varying degrees shouldn't be the milestones of a life. *There's so little time. I hope you're not wasting it.* Deep, deep down, I'd always had a nagging suspicion I was something special. Granted this inkling wasn't based on much, but still. I gaze down at Snap, Crackle and their cretinous friend, Pop. They gaze back. They're really pissing on my bonfire today.

I know this is the best of all worlds, that outside my door infinite possibility awaits. I know that great people have overcome huge obstacles, physical, mental and circumstantial to achieve

18

tremendous things. Andrew Ridgely convinced George Michael for years that leaving Wham and going solo would be a mistake. Knowing this isn't a relief. It means that it's my fault that my life is utterly vacuous. Being self-aware is really hard work when you're useless.

There's no excuse for boredom in this big world. There's a thousand years of literature to read, an entire decade of 80s films to watch and seven billion people to talk to. If you find them all boring, you're the problem. I find them all boring. I am the problem. This isn't the kind of problem that can be fixed with a montage. The heroic saga of a man overcoming tedium just isn't epic. The film adaptation won't star Gerard Butler or feature a rousing John Williams or Hans Zimmer score. It's really hard work being edgy when you're pointless.

Sitting here having a staring match with Pop because Snap and Crackle are too intimidating right now, I decide to become a man of action. If Lance Armstrong, the drug addict cyclist could win the Tour de France four times *and* walk on the moon, I can think my way out of being a loser. But, even the most proactive people wait for happiness to happen to them. Native Americans would dance about to influence the weather, but happiness is left to happen organically. Where do you even start? I could make a project of it. If nothing else, I'm a man of many side projects. It might be time for a main project. No more procrastination.

Procrastination

The word procrastination has lofty, literary allusions to Shakespeare and Prince Hamlet. It sounds noble and a bit sexy. Being a useless prick is a perfectly serviceable synonym.

No more. I'll push it to the max, lick the envelope, not live on the edge, but jump off it and various other motivational banal, cliché, platitude bromides. I'll be a soldier of fortune. I'll answer the door to Jehovah witnesses, try sushi, get in a fist fight and maybe even track down The Swan. (I'll fill you in about The Swan in a bit). No! That won't be enough. I want to be sure I never have another day like this one ever again and I'm excruciatingly aware how much of a flaker I am. Seeing that this is a terrible time to under react, I resign myself. Over reacting is highly underrated. I'll have to do something irrevocable. Live full time in a hot air balloon? Maybe join the foreign legion? To forget. Was there much that I want to forget? I'm not so much haunted by the past as taunted by the present. Does the foreign legion offer assistance with that sort of thing? I'm not a big fan of the French. This life changing epiphany is interrupted by the phone ringing. Thank Christ! I wouldn't normally answer it, but I could really use a break from myself.

"Hello?"

"Alright?" It's Hotdog.

"Alright. How are the legs?

"- Salmon jumping up waterfalls

- Foreign people who learn incredibly regionally specific yet still heavily accented English

- Indiana Jones' punch sound effect"

"That bad huh?"

"They're still pretty sore. It's the itchiness that's killing me and I can't scratch them with the bloody casts. It's driving me mental."

"Any news from work?"

"Mate. They offered me thirty grand if I agree to settle immediately."

"Jesus! And?"

"And I settled. Immediately."

"Wow! What are you gonna do?"

"Well, I've spent the last two weeks on the sofa watching The Antiques Roadshow with my dad."

"OK?"

"Well, it turns out I have quite the eye for guessing how much stuff is worth."

"OK?"

"I've decided to use the money to start investing in antiques, art and memorabilia."

"OK." Normally, a friend would constructively crush their pal's dream at this point for their own good but in my current mindset, any kind of action seems like a brilliant idea.

"Listen. I have to tell you something." Hotdog says, "I've decided to stay on at home permanently, for a little while."

"OK?"

"Obviously, I'll keep up with the rent until you find someone. I just want to save a bit and maybe get my own place once the business takes off."

"OK. Wait! What business?"

"The antiques business."

"Oh! That's fine. I'm sure I'll find someone no problem."

"Yeah? You're not annoyed?"

"As long as you're happy."

"Thanks. I'll come and get my stuff when I'm a bit more mobile."

"No worries. Talk to you later." I hang up.

That fucker! First, he drags me into that den of death and now this? Permanently, for a little while. The kid is a walking, talking contradiction. Well, not walking. I know what this is about too.

He'd been acting odd for two weeks before his accident. Hotdog is as homophobic as he is colour blind and he suffers from the very rare and most severe form of colour blindness. It's called Monochromacy. He doesn't just have an issue with mixing up blues and reds, he actually sees in black and white. To Hotdog, sunsets are rubbish, and he has no idea how brilliant Oz is compared to Kansas. It's a legitimate medical condition, but everyone thinks it's hilarious.

His toothbrush is blue. Mine is red. When we realised we'd both accidentally been using the same one for over a month, he went all weird, despite the fact that we've been best friends for over twenty-five years. Hotdog's parents are extremely religious, and they've poured enough Catholic guilt, shame and rage into him to poison a whole Mardi Gras parade. He is a terrible bigot, but I just can't bring myself to hold it against him.

God help me, I need a new flat mate. I'll need to take action, and then, against all odds, I do. So, suddenly, defying gravity, I put my trousers on. Overcoming adversity like a champion, I leave the house. I go to the library to use their Interweb. Of course, the only people there are serial killers in coats with furry hoods and people printing off boarding passes. The only thing worse than dying alone is strangers from the Interweb but I write up an ad about the vacant room, pray for sanity and press submit. Within a couple of hours of forcing myself to answer phone calls to strangers, and filtering out the taxidermists, ventriloquists and taxidermist-ventriloquists, I have three viewings set for tomorrow.

Next, I set about cleaning the flat. I put all the dirty dishes in the freezer, cryogenically freezing them for the archaeologists of the future to worry about. Then, I tackle the bathroom. Mopping the floor goes OK but I've never cleaned a shower before. I briefly consider doing it naked but think better of it. I want to save bleaching my pubes for later on in my midlife crisis. The Pesto Chick once said that there was an excellent chance I was cultivating smallpox in my old flat. I told her not to worry because I was growing penicillin too. She'd laughed. I'd always felt five foot eleven tall whenever I made her laugh. I swallow this thought and throw everything that isn't nailed down into black plastic bin bags and then, lurking in the shadows like a janitorial ninja under the cloak of darkness, throw them on top of the pile the neighbourhood kids are building for the annual bonfire. When I get home, I perform a Febreze exorcism on the place and go to bed.

Viewings

I wake up to the alarm shrieking at the crack of noon. It's ten past before I go and urinate with 98.9 percent accuracy. Not great, but still infinitely better than the infamous Sneeze Piss of Spring '17. I do five hundred sit-ups, one hundred push-ups and fifty pull-ups. I shovel down Rice Krispies from an old flowerpot and wait for the maniacs to descend upon me.

The first loon to darken my doorway (Sloppy Joe) is about forty-five, with a ponytail, a leather waist coat and KISS KISS tattooed across his knuckles. The menacing effect is somewhat dampened by having LOST BOYS tattooed lower down his fingers so that his left hand reads KISS BOYS. We shake hands and I notice his fingernails. There is something incredibly disturbing about a grown man with long nails if he isn't wearing an evening dress.

I invite him in, and he tells me he's the sound engineer for a Status Quo tribute band and he'd be on the road most of the time.

Status Quo
Status Quo are a guitar band from the 70s. They're rubbish!

This sounds promising until he adds that he'd need some of the living room as well as the spare bedroom to display his collection of samurai swords, knives, nun-chucks and throwing stars. He also owns a professional massage table which takes up a lot of space.

"Do you know much about the healing power of crystals?"

"Probably not as much as you." I say cautiously.

"You'd be amazed by the results."

"I would?" I definitely wouldn't.

"Absolutely. I know a woman who was getting poisoned by chemotherapy. It didn't help at all. Then, she started using crystals and suddenly her cancer went into remission and eventually clearly up altogether."

"Did she stop getting the chemo when she started using the crystals?"

"What?"

"Thanks for stopping by."

The second lunatic (Rare Beef and Rocket) is a Scottish guy wearing a kilt on a Wednesday afternoon in September. Beef Rocket has Day of The Dead tattoos covering his arms and legs and a Mac 3 shaved head in a transparent attempt to conceal gingerness. He seems more eccentric than deranged though. He's a travelling sales rep and one of those Scots that no matter what they're saying, sounds like they're about to club you to death. I ask him about the mid-week kilt, and he says he's playing golf later, as if that explains anything. It's all going OK until Beef Rocket goes to "Take a fucking piss like".

As he comes out of the bathroom, he leaves a trail of droplets behind him on the lino that Hansel and fucking Gretel could have followed all the way home. The flip-flop policy now indefinitely extends to the living room too.

The next time I hear a knock on the door, I open it and a gasp escapes my lips. The third psycho (Puppies and Coleslaw) instantly has the door slammed in his face. I triple lock it. He bangs on the door.

"I'm sorry. The room's been taken." I shout through the door.

The banging stops. Thank God for that bloody Swan! Puppies and fucking coleslaw? How did it ever come to this? I guess I better tell you. Plus, I've mentioned The Swan three times now with no explanation. Get ready for a long-distance flashback. We're going all the way back to a time of baggy jeans, centre parting haircuts and pop music so bad that even after nearly twenty-five years, people are still struggling to feel nostalgic towards it.

Apples and Peers

I may have always suspected I was something special, but the only extraordinary thing about me is my sixth sense. I got it when I was twelve. It was the end of August, and I'd been looting the nuns' orchard with the lads (Hotdog, Bangers, and Rasher). This was always one of the highlights of the calendar year, somewhere between Easter and Christmas, both chronologically and in order of importance. It was as dangerous as it was delicious.

The orchard was behind the local nunnery. The nuns, or Birds of Pray as we called them, weren't a problem. Nuns not only resemble penguins, they're also pretty cumbersome on land. Maybe they're brilliant swimmers? I'll get back to you on that. But the security guard was another story. Every child within ten miles was terrified of him. I can't remember what he looked like now, so I just picture him as The Child Catcher from *Chitty Chitty Bang Bang* as he hunted the orchard thieves.

Chitty Chitty Bang Bang
Chitty Chitty Bang Bang is a 1968 British musical-fantasy film by Roald Dahl and Ian Fleming. It stars Dick Van Dyke. It's brilliant!

The security guard may or may not have had a giant net on a stick. He probably definitely did. Running this fruity gauntlet required stealth, courage and an insatiable appetite for fresh fruit. The stakes were high but there's very little in life sweeter than an apple you've ripped directly from the tree while trespassing on private property. You can taste the sunshine, and the larceny.

If you were feeling generous, you could say that robbing those nuns was our first act of rebellion against the last, tenuous grip of the Catholic Church. You would have to be feeling very generous though. The real crime would have been not to steal those apples. Nearly as egregious as walking past a swimming pool without a cannon ball.

In hind-spite, it's pretty obvious the security guard was just the groundskeeper, and he was more worried about young savages falling out of trees and breaking their necks than thwarting our efforts to steal a few apples. This wasn't obvious at the time however. At the time, he was a tyrant, I was Robin Hood and Hotdog, Bangers, and Rasher were my Merry Men.

It must have been his day off because we got quite the haul that hot day in August. I was the best climber. I could scale anything back then or get an apple off the highest branch of any tree. Fear only found me at the very top of whatever I was climbing, at which point I'd be stuck until boredom outweighed terror. Rasher had a different technique. He'd climb halfway up a tree and start shaking it until Paula Red, Pacific Rose or Granny Smiths fell from the sky like a fruity apocalypse.

We were walking home by the river, ripping the piss out of Bangers as he lied about kissing a girl he'd met on his holidays. We were ninety-nine percent sure he was lying through his teeth, but we wanted that last one percent. The thought of being left behind in childhood while that idiot stumbled his way into adolescence wasn't to be countenanced. None of us were quite ready to give up sword fighting with sticks either though. Twelve is a funny age. While Bangers swore on his life he'd seduced her with the smooth line "Nice jeans. Wanna can of Coke?", it struck.

All of a sudden, it came at us out of nowhere. The biggest Swan you've ever seen. Even now, over twenty years later, that's the official story. All of a sudden, The Swan came at us out of nowhere. They'll all vouch for it. Actually, we'd been throwing Granny Smiths at it before it reared up like a fucking T-Rex and charged, its eyes filled with rabies rage, not quite flying but with wings outstretched for menacing effect. As we made to flee, I tripped on one of Rasher's dropped apples and tumbled to the ground. The lads dived over a ditch, leaving me for dead. Robin Hood must have had a stricter vetting process when he picked his Merry Men.

The Swan crashed over me like a white, flappy wave. Darwin was right. That feathery fuck definitely evolved from a dinosaur and just as my mother (Turkey and Stuffing) had warned me a thousand times, The Swan broke my arm with its wing. She hadn't mentioned it might peck me as well.

I passed out through either pain or terror and when I came to, I was in hospital demented on painkillers. There was a cast on my left arm and two stitches an inch from my jugular. My mother was hovering over me, smug, clearly impatient to rub it in. I hadn't believed her about swans breaking arms, but it had been a needle of truth in a haystack of deceit. She's a pathological liar, my mother. She made some pretty outrageous health and safety claims when I was a kid. She convinced me a splinter that didn't come out straight away would burrow into my veins, race to my heart and kill me. Her list of everyday life hazards was endless;

- Swallowing chewing gum would kill me
- Eating before swimming would kill me
- Earwigs wanted nothing but to get into my ear, burrow into my brain and kill me
- A hamster would kill me
- If lightning didn't kill me, quicksand would
- Daddy longlegs are more poisonous than tarantulas
- Watching a bit of *Postman Pat* would make me go blind
- Absolutely everything was haunted

The jury amongst the scientific community is still out regarding the thermodynamic assertion that "You won't feel the benefit of that coat when you go back out" if you don't instantly strip out of a jacket upon crossing a threshold. To be honest, I'm still half convinced about that one.

Over the next couple of days, something started coming to me. Once it started, it's never stopped, like a supernatural tennis ball to the face. Wanted or not, blessing or curse, whenever I encounter another human being, I instantly know what their favourite sandwich is. I've got Psychic Sandwich Rabies. I'm pretty sure it was The Swan. Or maybe those bloody nuns knew Voodoo. Either way, it's rubbish and Professor X still hasn't been in touch.

This sandwich thing doesn't come in handy nearly as much as you might think. I thought about becoming a chef. Somehow, I make a brilliant sandwich, but my culinary gusto only ever manifests itself between two slices of bread. I can't even fry an egg if it isn't going in a sandwich, and at the end of the day, a sandwich is never more than a sandwich, even if you sprinkle some parsley on top. Maybe the reason most people never try their best is because there's always an excellent chance it might amount to nothing more than hors d'oeuvres? I guess it saved me today from a psychopath who eats puppies. And coleslaw.

That's the first part of the long version of how I ended up in this dive. The short version is that The Pesto Chick threw me out. Figuratively of course. She was in no condition to physically throw a shoe at the end. I'd seen to that. I hadn't known my own strength. I found out though. And so did she. I swallow this thought. In this world, only three things endure: shame, rage and pyramids. I swallow this thought too.

Brie

Having nowhere else to turn, I ended up on the vintage sofa of my friend (Brie & Fig Jam). Brie's one of those friends who occasionally embarrasses you into reluctantly becoming a slightly better person. She's a shabby lady and a sophisticated tramp. She's like a scruffy unicorn. Or a dirty phoenix. Or a rainbow during a high smog level alert. If you don't know what I mean, I can't make it any clearer.

She's been trying to explain to me for ten years now what feminism is, and for ten years I've been pretending not to get it. It infuriates her. It's hilarious. By day, I'd half-heartedly look for a flat and by night I'd help Brie drink all the wine while she tried to explain gender equality to me. I'd look thoughtful before asking questions about the difference between Black Widow Lesbians and Praying Mantis Lesbians. I ended up staying a little longer than intended, but Brie being the gracious host she is, would never even hint that I was beginning to overstay my welcome. There *are* things she would do however.

She came home after work one evening with a tiny kitten. Brie knew that I come from a long line of dog people that goes all the way back to the early days of trying to convince a wolf to fetch a stick, but the kitten and I were to be roommates. This was to be the cat's first night away from its cat mother and cat brothers and sisters. As soon as Brie said goodnight and closed her bedroom door, which happened to be the only door in the small flat, I turned to look at my new roommate. It seemed lonely and keen to be friends. I chased it out of the living room.

I switched the lights off and tried to get some sleep. The cat turned out to be more lonely than intimidated. Something woke me up by landing on my legs and frightening the bejesus out of me. The feline fucker wanted to spoon. I shooed it off the sofa and it jumped straight back up. I shooed it again and sure enough, up it came. This tiny, rubbish lion thought we were playing a game. This went on for bloody ages.

I woke in the morning to purring. I opened my eyes to find the cat on the back of the sofa, hovering four inches above my face, staring down at me. I'd found my new flat by noon and bullied Hotdog into moving in with me. A couple of weeks later, I learned Brie had returned the borrowed cat to its real owner by early evening. I foresee her running this country or starting her own someday.

And here I stand, six months later, barricaded inside this shabby hovel with nothing but three inches of wood to separate me from a maniac who eats puppy and coleslaw sandwiches. I really need to get out of this place. Wasn't I planning on doing something irrevocable? I decide to stop thinking so much and act on impulse. Do something reckless. But what? What do reckless people do? I could get caught up in the world of drugs? Get drunk on cocaine? At the very least, stealing tellies from the elderly and giving sailors hand jobs on the docks to pay for my next fix would pass the time and get me out of the house.

I call up my hippy friend (Beetroot & Feta) and ask him where he gets his drugs. He rings me back ten minutes later and tells me to meet Drug Dealer Jay at the bus stop outside the lesbian karaoke bar at 8.

The Bender

I sit at the bus stop shelter outside the lesbian karaoke bar. It's called Gash. I'm here twenty minutes and there's no sign of Drug Dealer Jay. Apparently, drug dealers are notoriously unreliable. Then I notice a guy (Peanut Butter) in a hoodie and white tracksuit bottoms cycling towards me. PB Hoodie eyeballs me menacingly. Is this drug people code? I return the look uncertainly. It seems like he's just going to cycle right past, but he abruptly turns and slowly loops around the back of the bus shelter and comes back again looking at me. Then he circled again. And again. It's like a scene from *Jaws*.

"Are you . . . Are you Jay?" I mumble.

PB Hoodie screeches to a halt in front of me and just stares. Without a word, he nods at the lane across the street and leads the way. There's nothing to do but follow. This is finally starting to look like how it is on telly. It's a bit exciting actually. I follow him down a back alley off a back lane behind a back street and I'm wondering what type of drugs I should get when PB & Jay stops, gets off his bike and takes his dick out of his white track suit and says,

"You bet your sweet ass I'm gay."

Oh God! This guy wasn't PB & *Jay*. He was PB & *Gay*. Is this what adventure is? My heart pounds in my chest like a rabbit caught is sexually aggressive headlights.

"Listen there's been a huge misunderstanding. You mishea-" PB & Gay shoves me up against the wall and goes for my belt. All women everywhere were right. Men are pigs. I shove him back. PB & Gay trips over his BMX and lands on *his* sweet ass. I run for it. I get to the end of the back lane off the back alley behind the

33

backstreet and just keep running. I hear a bike catching up from behind. There's something else too.

"Duuuuuuuun, Dun . . ." What the actual fuck?

"Duuuuuuuun, Dun . . ." This fucker is indeed a sex predator, land Jaws.

"Dun-DUN-Dun-DUN" And the shark is gaining.

"DunDun-DunDun-DunDun-DunDun-DunDun"

I run until I can't. Then I canter. Then I trot. After that, I briefly jog. When I exhaust my lungs and the concept of jogging, there's only one option left to me faster than walking. I skip. The sheer indignity!

Skipping
With the sole exception of escorting a young lady along the yellow brick road to the Emerald City, a grown man should never skip.

Then, like men fleeing their problems for countless generations before me, I pop into a pub. Bursting in, panting, I make quite the entrance. All conversation abruptly stops as everyone looks at me. Mumbling something lame about being chased by a dog, I'm instantly dismissed. I really need to stop mumbling. I won't be going back outside again any time soon, so I decide to have a drink. In hind-spite, I probably should've given getting caught up in the world of booze a whirl before making the leap to Class A drugs. I could be one of those mysterious, haunted, silent guys sitting at the bar, gazing into his drink looking for answers, trying to forget.

My eyes scan the room. I appear to have landed mid World War II. They even have black out curtains. There's a telly above the entrance and even though no one is watching it, the volume is so loud that Blackberry Jam could have heard it. The News is on and there's bombing and shooting going on in the Middle East. It's booming so loud I'm worried about PTSD.

The high ceilings give the place an old-fashioned vibe that's literally hard to put a finger on. The walls are all white with green trim and matching seats. A dartboard dominates the centre of the room with yellow crime scene tape on the floor in place of the throw line … which is called the … oche? There's a tiny stage on the other side wrapped in plastic covered in dust smothered in regret. This place hasn't seen a shindig in a good long while.

Directly ahead of the entrance, a rather distinguished older gentleman in shirt and tie (Corned Beef and Mustard) stands behind the bar looking as surprised to see me as I am to be there. I doubt he gets many scruffy, beardy weirdos in here. Three gentlemen and a lady play cards at the end of the bar. I'm the only one in here too young to have helped build Stonehenge.

I order a lager, but the gas needs changing, and the beer trickles out like sand through an hourglass. When you're a man circling around the drain of a nervous breakdown, everything starts to look like sand through an hourglass. The barkeep has the patience of a Buddhist monk however, and clearly has no intention of changing the tank. I won't lie. It's awkward. I watch the flat lager dribble into the glass, and I start to think about the past. And the future. *There's so little time. I hope you're not wasting it.*

At the quarter way point, I consider asking for a bottle instead, but I've lost all confidence. I'm on the cusp of a full-blown meltdown before the glass is half full. Or is it half empty? I honestly don't know. I should have gone for hard liquor. There's a strange array of bottles on the optics. I've never seen apple sours or Pernod upside down before. Martini and a type of rum I've not heard of are on offer for a quid. I should have gotten a Martini to

35

take the edge off. I down my beer and risk the run to the pub next door before the time streams realign and I get trapped in the 1940s forever. There's no sign of PB & Gay outside.

This new place is reassuringly dingy. I find a barstool and the barman (Hawaiian Toasty) asks what I'm having. Deciding to loosen the reigns on my OCD a little, I start drinking alphabetically with an **A**maretto. Then a **B**aileys. And a **C**ointreau. Then a **D**rambuie. The whole mysterious, haunted, silent guy thing goes straight out the window as all of a sudden, I can't quite seem to shut the fuck up. For some reason, I'm telling the barman that swans can live to be thirty years old, Hawaiian Toasty couldn't be less interested.

After he begrudgingly makes me an **E**spresso Martini, the chronological record skips and I notice I have a **G**in in front of me. The record skips again and I'm in another bar with a **H**ennessy in my hand. I assume I had a **J**ameson somewhere? I hear myself ordering an IPA. *SKIP.*

I'm sitting at a table in a different bar with a **K**ahlua and a **L**ong Island. I appear to have made friends. *SKIP.*

I seem to have lost the power of speech. I'm floating from one group to another listening to conversations, neither adding nor contesting anything. *SKIP.*

I'm standing around a bonfire in what looks like a gypsy halting site. I've got a bottle of **N**ewcastle Brown Ale in one hand and a pair of rusty pliers gripping a steak that's clearly been cooked on the bonfire in the other. I gnarl off a mouthful with the table manners of a caveman. It doesn't taste like cow. Through a mouthful of gristle, I appear to be in the middle of negotiating the price of a tortoise with a (Bacon and Cabbage) gypsy. I'm as surprised as ol' Cabbage Sandwiches is to hear myself claiming to be no fool when it comes to buying exotic reptiles and I demand

36

Cabbage half what he's asking for it. **SKIP**.

I'm face down on the living room floor at home. I'm sure I can smell piss mixed with Irn Bru. Am I lying in Scottish piss? Two cardboard boxes lie open beside me. They have air holes in them.

I push up from the floor. Feathers and blood litter the whole place like wedding confetti. A rooster struts out of the bathroom. I find another dead in the kitchen. Have I held an illegal cock fight in the flat? I check the clock. How is it only eleven o'clock? The rooster's looking at me funny. I stumble for the door. **SKIP**.

I'm pissing like a racehorse at a quirky urinal and chatting to some girl (Nutella).

"I really don't know how I feel about these unisex toilets. Maybe I'm old fashioned, but it feels inappropriate to be urinating in front of you like this." I say gallantly.

Nutella Girl rolls her eyes, with hands on her hip and says, "This is the ladies' mate. You're pissing in the sink." **SKIP**.

I'm holding what smells like **P**each Schnapps in what I think is Gash. I'm at the bar talking to a really buff, turbo camp black guy (Meat Lovers) about singing. Meat Lover is telling me how his grandmother prayed to God one night that he would be an amazing singer, and the very next day, he was. I'm only half listening as I'm trying to think of a drink that begins with the letter **Q**. I ask Meat Lover if he wants a **Q**uick Fuck. He looks embarrassed and says something sheepish, but I'm already ordering and not paying attention. **SKIP**.

I've got a **R**um in one hand and a microphone in the other. I'm arm in arm with Meat Lover and we're halfway through "Ebony and Ivory". Meat Lover is doing the ivory part and I'm doing the ebony bit. I'm not sure if this was a mistake or if we're being profound. Either way, Meat Lover's grandmother needs to keep praying. He's got the voice of a dancer. **SKIP**.

37

Kissing. Panic. Girl (Spicy Chicken). Relief. Pretty girl. Pleasantly surprised. **SKIP.**

Still kissing. (Tuna Mayo). Not same girl. Not as pretty. A drag queen (Cucumber Triangles) is tapping me on the shoulder. She doesn't have an Adam's apple. It's a fucking pineapple! She's telling me what we're doing is disgusting and it's Adam and Steve here, not Adam and Eve. I hear myself indignantly saying that we're not hurting anyone and that it feels natural to us. **SKIP.**

I'm in another bar. Looking around, I have no idea where I am. There's a White Russian in my hand and I'm sitting under a black light. The drink looks radioactive but, on the upside, I seem capable of conscious thought again. There's a guy sitting beside me at the next table eyeballing me. Every time I check in the corner of my eye, he's looking at me. I'm uncomfortable but in a cosy, boozy way. Maybe I should leave? No! This is the perfect time to get into a fight. A bar brawl. A fracas. Like in a Clint Eastwood film. I sit there trying to summon my inner lioness and every time I turn to check, this dickhead is staring at me.

I let go of the ball of anger that lives in the centre of me. All of my frustrations bubble to the surface. Springing to my feet, I manage not to fall over just as this dickhead gets up too. Someone, somewhere, almost certainly a terrible 80s action film, once said the one to strikes first, strikes last. Right now, this seems like solid advice, so I lash out my best impression of a punch in the general direction of my foe. I'm already not paying attention before my fist lands. Fright and confusion jolt me back as the whole world explodes in my face. No, not the world, a floor to ceiling mirror. I've been catching glimpses of myself catching glimpses of myself for God only knows how long. I'm not too drunk to be disgusted with myself. No matter where I go, there I am. Fuck! **SKIP.**

Oblivion. Then pulsing. Every time it pulses, my brain and my hand scream. I lie there hoping I'll just go away. I never go away. I'll have to investigate. I chance a sniff. Wherever I am, it smells like piss, but not the familiar Scottish kind. Advancing my fingers, it feels like I'm lying on rough wood. I open one eye just enough to let some light in. My vision clears and I look around. I'm in a room with two men (Wensleydale /Club) asleep on benches, snoring loudly. Christ! Have I been arrested? I'm wearing navy overalls and there's a huge bandage around my hand. My hands are filthy. The other two aren't wearing overalls. What have I done? Sitting up, the agony of the pulsing multiplies by ten. I wait for it to pass. A juice box has been left by my head. How have I only just noticed how thirsty I am? I shive? No, shank, definitely shank, the top of the juice box with the straw (mastering prison lingo is essential if you're gonna make it on the inside). I chug the warm, sour juice. It's delicious. Then, I quietly tip toe over to my two unconscious cellies and steal their drinks too. I hide the empty cartons under my bench and lie back down. I feel like death. "Never again." I whisper.

The Never Again
The hungover "Never Again" is bullshit, but it's load bearing bullshit. We'd crumble without it.

The Pesto Chick used to wake up like this all the time. She was a much bigger drinker than me. She'd get so hungover, she'd change colours. But even when she was green, she was gorgeous, like a sexy She-Hulk. She woul- **SKIP**.

I wake up to shouting. There's a policewoman (B.L.T) standing over me. I'm led like a farmyard animal out of the cell and into an interview room. She plants me across from two policemen

39

(Bacon/Brown Sauce, Bacon/Ketchup). I'm too hungover to be amused by the piggy coincidence.

"Good morning sir." Ketchup says with exaggerated civility.

"Hello." To say I'm sheepish would be bluster at this stage.

"And how are you feeling today?"

"Not very well." I whisper.

"That's to be expected after the evening you had. Good night, was it?"

"Erm, yes?"

"Do you remember what you got up to?"

"To be honest, I don't." I sigh.

"You. my friend, were arrested for criminal damage. You broke a mirror."

"Oh! Yeah." Fuck!

"Oh? Yeah? The landlord held you until officers arrived to escort you to the station."

"The landlord held me? Like a citizen's arrest? Is that really a thing? Isn't it a bit of a grey area between a citizen's arrest and just kidnapping someone?"

"Focus!" Brown Sauce snaps.

"Yeah. Sorry. Yeah."

"The landlord is willing to forego pressing charges if you cover the cost of the damages."

"Of course. Yeah. Of course." I eagerly agree.

"Good. You're lucky. He reckoned it was too funny to hold a grudge. He said he'd never seen a man hate himself so much that it came to blows before. Now, this leads us to the other matter." Oh God! What?

"Do you know why you're wearing those overalls?"

"I was wondering."

40

"The only way we could stop you shouting that you needed to be 'finished off by a **Z**ombie' was to let you have 'the full authentic prison experience' and give you a jump suit. You then proceeded to break a pen and left inky fingerprints all over the reception area."

"That really doesn't sound like me. I'm really very sorry"

"Son, you were on autopilot, and on autopilot, everyone's a monster."

"I'm really very sorry. I was so drunk I couldn't even talk."

"Oh, you could talk alright. You just couldn't listen." says Brown Sauce.

"Erm, yeah."

"Never waste police time again."

"Yes sir. Absolutely."

They get up and walk out. As soon as the door closes, I hear them erupt into bellowing gales of laughter. Of course. Two minutes later, B.L.T comes in with my clothes and takes my information. In my pocket, I find a rabbit's foot that I'd probably gotten from the gypsies and a phone number for someone called Winston with threes kisses and "Call me" written underneath the digits. Meat Lover?

I'm released and shamble home. I get about halfway there when I stop in my tracks. There's a fucking homicidal rooster in the flat! I know I should do something about him when I get home but having to clean up one feathery, blood bath massacre is as much carnage as I can handle. If I had to kill my own animals, it'd be me, Rooster, a cow and a pig living in the flat, eating beans on toast together forever. I put the dead rooster in the freezer with the dirty dishes. Maybe one day, cryogenic scientists can bring him back. Then, I do forty sit-ups, thirty push-ups, vomit, eight pull-ups. Then, I vomit and cry in the shower before passing out.

The next morning, I'm yanked out of a bad dream by Rooster cock-a-doodle-doo-ing at the foot of my bed. He frightens the life out of me. It's literally the crack of dawn. I chase him out into the living room and throw a copy of War and Peace at him.

"Cock-a-doodle-don't!" I shout.

Rooster retreats to the kitchen. I go to the bathroom and urinate with 99.3% accuracy. My piss looks like Fanta. I need to rehydrate. Booze is not my friend. It costs too much. Emotionally.

I go back to bed. When I eventually get up, Rooster is rummaging about the flat. He must be hungry, but the cock won't eat Rice Krispies. It's only when I'm at the register of the supermarket paying Pork Belly for a loaf of wholemeal bread that I realise what I'm doing. I'm running errands for that murderous, beaky prick.

It's an unseasonably nice day and I don't want to go home, so I go for a walk in the park. After performing an extensive reconnaissance to make sure there's no swans in the vicinity of the pond, I feed the ducks most of Rooster's lunch. I wonder over to the playground and try to have a go on the seesaw, but it's rubbish by myself. It's not nearly as rubbish as eating an ice cream on the swings though. It gets bloody everywhere, and I've got one nipple as sharp as a knife. Upon hearing the school bells letting out in the distance, I realise I'm a grown man with one pointy nipple, hanging about a playground by myself, so I promptly evacuate the area before I get arrested again.

The thought of facing Rooster with that murderous look in his eye is just too intimidating right now, so I go to a quiet corner at the other side of the pond. It's a picturesque park, full of mounds and little hills. I sit on a grassy knoll and take an apple out of my backpack and put it down beside me. It instantly rolls down the bank, and faster than I can curse Isaac Newton's name or be bothered to go get it, a seagull swoops down like a fucking fighter jet and pecks it, effectively calling avian dibs. Fucking birds! This never would have happened with a Twix ... maybe with a Chocolate Orange. Grassy knolls absolutely deserve their bad rep. I watch the squirrels for a while before lying back to look at the clouds. Eventually, I fall asleep. The sensation of my face being on fire wakes me up hours later. Sunburn. In fucking September!

I stop at the chemist on the way home to buy after sun. I'm just leaving when I get a call on my portable telephone from Hotdog. He tells me that Rasher's dad has died and asks if I'll come to the funeral with him. I tell him of course I will. Rooster is waiting for me when I get home. Anyone who doesn't think that an animal can have enough personality to be a dickhead is both under and overestimating them. This guy is sinister as fuck. I throw the bread at him, and he pounces on it. My eyes never leave the feathery savage as I coat myself in two inches of after sun. Eventually, it's gonna be either me or him. I'm not as confident as I'd like.

The Funeral

Rooster loses his mind at dawn again and almost gets decapitated by a copy of Don Quixote. I stumble into the bathroom and am pissing with pretty good accuracy until I peer in the mirror and jump and piss all over the place. And myself. Not recognising yourself twice in four days would be really worrying if there hadn't been a fucking Umpa Lumpa gaping back at me. I pick up the bottle on the sink. On closer inspection, it wasn't after sun at all. It was a moisturising fake tan. The directions advise to apply lightly and evenly and rinse off after twenty minutes. I'd massaged it into my face and arms every twenty minutes for hours last night and I hadn't showered before bed. This would have been horrendous even if I hadn't already had a glow in the dark radioactive sunburn. I have to be at a funeral in a few hours. I get in the shower and start scrubbing furiously. It's beyond hopeless. I'm fit for nothing other than factory labour and singing rhyming cautionary fables to horrible children.

I'm ironing my suit on a surfboard when Hotdog hops up on crutches. With his colour blindness, he doesn't notice that I've been Tangoed. To top it off, he's wearing his funeral suit. He bought it last year for his uncle's funeral. He was so upset about his uncle dying that no one had the heart to tell him it was dark purple, so this funeral is about to have a Willy Wonka and an Umpa Lumpa combo in attendance. I insist we arrive late, so we sip tea from a test tube and a bell jar because there's no clean mugs. I plan for us to join the end of the funeral parade on its way from the funeral home to the church like when The Scarecrow, Tinman & Cowardly Lion joined the end of the Wicked Witch's security patrol.

Ohh-Eee-Ooohh-Eeeee-Ooooohhhh-Oohh.

The funeral home is at the bottom of my street. People notice our arrival. Rasher's dad was old, so though it's a sad affair, it's not tragic. The more casual mourners at the back are snickering. This constant deluge of major and minor humiliations must surely take its toll eventually? As usual, Hotdog is completely oblivious. There's a good turnout. Rasher's dad was well liked and more importantly, it's a nice day. The attendance of one's funeral is less a testament of their character and the mark they've made on the world than an accurate gage of that particular day's weather. Our old friend Bangers makes his way over to us and we march on together.

"What the fuck? Is this funeral fancy dress? Nobody bloody told me." he whispers in earnest.

"There's no such fucking thing as a fancy-dress funeral." I quietly roar at him. Hotdog asks what we're talking about, but I tell him to shut up and show some respect. At the church, Holy Guacamole is performing the mass, but all the bloody prayers have changed since I last worshipped. Why is a two-thousand-year-old religion mixing things up now? There's a smug, God suck-up in the row behind us (Branston/Cheddar) shouting out the new responses and a woman in front of us with Tuberculous (Cold Roast Lamb) is trying to cough a lung into her hand. She has a hanky. An honest to God hanky A.K.A a booger bandana AKA a snot scarf AKA a phlegm pashmina. In this fucking day and age! I know she's going to want to shake my hand during the "Offer each other the sign of peace" bit in ten minutes and I'm utterly powerless to get out of it.

45

"Offer Each Other The Sign of Peace"

More than the advent of science, scandal, corruption, and the church losing power to secularism, nothing has turned people away from religion more than that awkward bit during mass when you have to shake hands with people you'd successfully ignored for the previous forty minutes.

I fume as I shake germy hands with The Lamb of God and say "How are you?" The old waif holds my hand and my eye and pointedly says "Peace be with you." I've never cared for lamb.

I make Hotdog hang back as everyone makes their way out of the church before the hike to the graveyard. I tell him I want to light a candle for Rasher's dad. He still has no idea about the state we're in. We go to the candle station area at the back of the church, and as slowly as possible, I light five candles. Hotdog looks all contemplative and is probably praying. I fake likewise until I zone out. I inhale deeply and am about to exhale when Hotdog's hand covers my mouth.

"What the fuck are you doing?" he whispers.

"Nothing."

"Were you about to blow out those candles?"

"No. I was praying."

"You were wishing, you fucker! Get out that door before me."

"Don't curse in the church." I chide him and walk ahead before he loses his mind.

After a thousand years and two thousand miles, the funeral procession (it's definitely not called a parade) gets to the graveyard. Instead of listening to Holy Guacamole as he mindlessly chants the rosary by the grave, I think about Rasher's dad. He was a good man. He always had mints. He was a heavy drinker and his liver failed. I'm not paying the slightest bit of attention to Holy Guacamole, but halfway through his sermon, he spots me. All of a sudden, the whole vibe of the funeral changes direction and Holy Guacamole is urging anyone with or anyone who knows someone with a drinking problem to seek help. All this seems to be aimed at me for some reason. I'm baffled by this until it hits me. No fucking way! He thinks I have jaundice.

After an age, the coffin is lowered. Rasher, his mother (Tuna Mayo) and sister (Chorizo & Gouda) stand before the grave and people line up to pay their respects. I want to just leave but Hotdog, still oblivious, throws a dirty look at me that makes me feel like I'm eight years old.

After everyone else has stepped aside, Hotdog leads the way. We both shake hands with Rasher's mother and sister who won't release her vice-like grip of my hand until I promise to get help. I'll go along with anything at this point. Then, we walk over to Rasher who just looks bewildered.

"I'm really sorry about your dad pal." Hotdog says.

"Yeah, He was a gentleman." I agree.

Rasher looks too intrigued to receive our condolences.

"Is this like a bad joke or something?" He's too puzzled to be furious.

I sigh and quickly explain what happened with the fake tan. Rasher laughs so hard, he nearly falls into the grave on top of his departed father. Laughter can be a great release during the mourning process. Maybe I'll humiliate myself again later for his amusement. It's the least I can do. Hotdog is beside himself.

A Tortuous Conversation with The Priest

Hotdog, Bangers and I are awkwardly standing about outside the graveyard gates having no idea what we're supposed to be doing when the priest approaches us. After the bare minimum of preamble, he launches straight in.

"How are you holding up boys? People often find their way to God through grief."

Before Hotdog can agree and prevent a scene which would be vastly unsatisfying, I decide to field this one.

"He'll have to come looking for us Father."

"He's always just outside. It's up to you to open the door."

"Let's not start talking in parables Father."

"He *is* the only way to eternal life." Holy Guacamole insists.

"Well . . ." I start.

"You've found another way?" he challenges.

"Well . . ."

"Do tell."

At this point, Hotdog is as red as I am orange and shaking his head wildly, but I've had a rough few days and decide to treat myself.

"OK. Since you asked. I might write a book, pour my blood, sweat and tears into it, print a hundred copies, seal them in lead boxes and bury them in the deepest cave systems around the world, in a glacier and bribe the night watchmen at the pyramids in Egypt and Mexico and the seed vault on Svalbard to hide copies in them, ensuring my work outlasts human civilisation."

"That's hardly eternal life. And what's the point if there's no one left to read it? There's a poem by Shelle-"

48

"Don't Ozymandias me Father. I'm not finished. When alien archaeologists discover one, if they find my prose compelling and my character arcs engaging, they can bring me back. That's what all the blood, sweat and tears are for. DNA."

"Semen?" asks Bangers.

"Maybe semen." I agree. At this point the vein pulsing on the side of Holy Guacamole's forehead to tapping out GO FUCK YOURSELF in Morse code.

"A hundred books? You'll need a lot of semen." Bangers continues.

"There's no problem there pal."

"I see you've put a great deal of thought into this." Holy Guacamole says through gritted teeth.

"Shame, rage and pyramids Father."

"What?" asks the priest.

"Never mind."

"Excuse me boys." He says as he storms off.

"Yeah, God bless." Bangers says loudly to his back.

Hotdog turns on us, his arms folded in disgust.

"I can not believe you two just did that."

"Where's your faith pal?" says Bangers between chuckles "Look, it's not the 50s. He can't banish us or commit us to a mental institution.".

"Yeah. Fuck him." I add "Going about trying to indoctrinate people when they're vulnerable and facing their mortality. If this was even thirty years ago, he'd get us sacked and evicted. Don't think he isn't raging he's lost the option."

"You can't just judge people and things because of their pasts." Hotdog protests.

"What are you talking about? I say. "That's the only way to judge people."

"And things." adds Bangers.

"Your problem is, you always think your opinions are right." says Hotdog.

"What? If we didn't think they were right, they wouldn't be our opinions, would they?" I point out.

Afterwards there's drinks at the pub. Eventually, Rasher has enough booze in him so he can feel his feelings. He starts talking about his dad.

"Since he died, I've been thinking about when I was really little. I remember one time, he brought me to a park somewhere. Just me and him. It had this beautiful stream running through the centre of it and there were these steppingstones to get from one side to the other. We spent ages swinging from a rope over the water. There were frogs there. I've no idea where it is and there's no one else in the whole world I can ask. I've suddenly got a hundred questions for him that no one else can answer. I had my whole life to ask." He trails off.

A conversation transpires between Hotdog and I conveyed entirely via eyebrows.

SAY SOMETHING

YOU SAY SOMETHING

YOU'RE BEYOND USELESS

I COULD TELL HIM HE CAN ASK HIM IN HEAVEN?

DON'T YOU FUCKING DARE!

"I'll get you a drink." I suggest helpfully and bolt to the bar. Later Rasher sings a couple of ballads for his dad to a completely silent pub. Rasher is one of those people who can randomly just sing like a classically trained baritone. I used to think this kinda thing was just pouring petrol onto a bonfire of heartache, but I've come to realise it stops the hard men from just swallowing their grief. None of the old-school proper men cried during the mass or at the grave, but suddenly they're all choking on the lumps in their manly throats and there isn't a dry eye in the house.

At home later, I'm left shaken by my friend's honest out-pour. After Rooster is safely contained in the bathroom, I put the kettle on and adjust the Rice Krispie box so I can give Snap a determined glare. I'm more sure than ever that overreacting is underrated. I need to do something proper irrevocable. I pour myself an upside-down rabbit shaped jelly mould of tea and vow to defrost the dirty dishes and do the washing up before it comes to putting a tea bag in my hot water bottle. I'm ten minutes into a staring match with Crackle and starting to consider becoming a Jehovah Witness while simultaneously worrying about getting a new flatmate when I have an honest to God revelation. I'll rob a bank! That's pretty irrevocable. People do it all the time though. The news just doesn't go on about it when the robbers get away with it. That'd send the wrong message to the public. I won't need a new flatmate. I'll be able to afford to become a recluse and completely remove myself from society if I want. There'll be dozens of urban legends about my mysterious past. I'll be like Keyser Söze mixed with Tyler Durden. Kids will think I'm a mad scientist. Or a Russian spy. Or a former Mafia boss in witness protection. Or a lonely hermit with no friends who never leaves the house.

Bananarmed Robbery

I'll use a gun shaped banana under my jacket and employ the plan I came up with when I was eleven. I'll rob the bank beside the river on Halloween wearing scuba gear underneath my clothes and jump off the bridge and swim to financial freedom, nay, financial liberation. There'll be a media frenzy. They'll call me The Scuba Raider. I don't know anything about money laundering, but money tumble drying should be straight forward enough. I won't go for the vault. The vault eats up too much time. I can get a second-hand wet suit and one of those James Bond style mini oxygen tanks. If they exist. Finding a suitably gun shaped banana might be an issue, but I've learned from numerous terrible action films that as well as not going for the vault, you should always stick to the plan, even if it literally just occurred to you seconds earlier.

I'm suddenly filled with a new and completely unmerited sense of confidence and accomplishment. Anything could happen yet. Waking up at quarter past Satan's balls with Rooster every morning means that the possibilities for productivity are endless. I take the batteries out of the alarm clock so now I can piss whenever I like.

The next morning and every morning after for the next three weeks, I'm in the local pool by eight o'clock and before long my technique progresses from drowning so slowly that I can get to the other side without dying to heavy boned novice. My life is suddenly an 80s film training montage. With a spring in my step, I go to the outdoor market every morning for weeks before Halloween obsessively scrutinising the fruit and veg stalls looking for a banana that's just right. More than one greengrocer now thinks I'm madder than a box of frogs. I'm constantly buying bananas to allay suspicion, but what's the nutritional value of buying seven bananas a week and leaving them in a cupboard until they decompose? Is it possible to get too much potassium?

One of the greengrocers though (Zesty Prawn) has taken a shine to me. She even insists on giving me a slightly wonky pumpkin to carve for Halloween. Zesty Prawn's quite pretty. Definitely prettier than I am handsome, and she's casually asked on several occasions what my plans for the evening are, always to be told that I have a lot on. I'm not lying when I tell Zesty that I have a lot on. As well as swimming and exercising, I've been working on a Jamaican accent for weeks. The Pesto Chick works at the bank now, and I don't want her to recognise my voice, so I'm watching *Cool Runnings* every day and listening to a Bob Marley's greatest hits tape on repeat night and day. The only thing I hate more than Bob Marley now is reggae that isn't Bob Marley. If I wasn't a man on the edge before I'd heard *Redemption Song* for the thousandth time, I bloody well am now. I heard she's going out with some German now. Ann Frank would be spinning in her grave. I swallow the thought.

Other than that, I'm feeling much better about everything since I've become a man with a plan. I beat a sixty-year-old woman (Chicken Salad) at the breaststroke who didn't know we were racing and can hold my breath for eighty-four seconds now. I feel like I'm joining in with life instead of just observing with my eyes closed. As well as maintaining my guilt and shame fuelled morning exercise regime, I've added another strict policy to my routine. Trousers every day. Anything could happen when you've got trousers on. You can really go places.

The scuba gear arrives and a few days later, Zesty reluctantly sells me a hideously deformed banana bent almost at a ninety-degree angle. I pick up a Darth Vader mask, figuring there was no one more menacing. I'm ready. So, on all hallows eve, with the wet suit hidden under a pair of maternity dungarees, I waddle my way to the bank at quarter to five. I've got my mask, mini oxygen tank and slightly squishy banana in my loot satchel.

I falter at the door. My stomach's full of butterflies and streams of sweat are flowing into tiny lakes around where the wetsuit clings or bunches up. Actually, isn't this more like an eleven-year old's daydream than a plan? Something in me crackles. No! I *am* a man of action, a soldier of fortune. If that junkie, Lance Armstrong could cycle on the moon, I can be a scuba raider. I *am* pride. I *am* power. I'm a bad-ass mother who don't take no crap from nobody. I'm not having Rice Krispies tomorrow. Tomorrow will be different.

Pesto Chicken

I was working as a waitress in a cocktail bar when I met her. Well, I was doing a few afternoons in a horrible, old pub. Intimacy had always made me uncomfortable before I met her. It never quite felt right. An adoring gaze never failed to make me squirm. Then, she came in (Chicken Pesto). I remember it like it was yesterday. If I live to be a hundred, I'll remember it like it was yesterday. I'd never seen anyone like her. Cheeks, rosy from the cold. She was beautiful. Stripey, multicoloured cotton gloves with the fingertips cut off. She was eating an apple. The sound of her great big chomps boomed like a thunderclap. It's the most wholesome, healthy sound in the world. She noticed the jar with the giant biscuits that was bizarrely always kept on the bar.

"Are these good?" she asked. I'd never sold one. I was pretty sure they were left there until they could get up and walk away by themselves.

"It really depends what time of the month it is." I said.

"Oh, I have a sweet tooth all the time."

The awkward silence which followed once we both realised what we'd said was long enough for a Jamaican Olympian to run sprints on. I was on the verge of panic when she laughed. It was a great laugh. Then she snorted. She's one of those girls who always snorts and always acts shocked every time it happens like it's never happened before. I gave her a biscuit. I'm pretty generous anyway, but with other peoples' stuff, I'm basically Robin Hood. She thanked me politely but without being grateful. Beautiful girls get free shit wherever they go. They're always utterly perplexed whenever they hear a rumour of a stranger not bending over backwards for someone.

Christ! She'd said something and was looking at me as though I should be laughing. Had she said something funny? The beautiful people weren't supposed to be funny. Being funny is the only compensation us bridge trolls have. I forced my transparent, fake laugh and started polishing a wine glass to steady myself.

"You should pop by my work. I'll sort you out with mate's rates." she said.

"Yeah? What bar do you work at?"

"Who said I work at a bar?" Was she being coy? Jesus! Was she flirting?

"Restaurant?"

"Nope."

"My psychic powers are pretty specific." I say

"I manage the sex toy shop around the corner."

The glass I was polishing exploded in my hands. Turns out, the latent remnants of Catholicism never really let you go. There was glass and blood everywhere.

"Oh my God! Are you OK?" She was horrified.

"I'm fine." I tried to play it cool. It's really hard to play it cool when there's glass and blood everywhere. I was mortified. All the blood that wasn't pumping out of my hand went straight to my face.

"I'm sorry. I didn't mean to make you uncomfortable."

"I'm not uncomfortable." I scrambled, "Not at all. I go in there all the time.".

"But" she hesitated, "I've never seen you before?"

"Oh! Yeah." Christ!

"Come here and let's get you cleaned up. Do you have a first-aid kit?"

The Pesto Chick stopped the bleeding and bandaged up the cut on my palm. She was all business and briskness. I knew it there

56

and then. I was fucked. It wasn't courage or hope that made me ask her. It was terror. Terror of never seeing her again. Courage was bypassed entirely. It was involuntary. What I blurted out was as much a surprise to me as it was to her.

"I'd really like to take you out … like not with a shotgun or anything."

She laughed that laugh again. Earning that laugh was already my main project in life. She'd later complain I wasn't ambitious enough. There was a spark in her eye. She just seemed so excited about life and the world. You could feel it radiating from her. Have you ever been invited to two New Year's Eve parties and no matter how good the one you go to is, you're sure the other one would have been better? I'd always felt like that. All the time. Until I met her. Then, whenever I was with her, I knew I was in the right place. I swallow this thought.

Bobsled Time

Feel the rhythm. I put my mask and gloves on. Feel the ride. I get the banana out and stuff it up my jumper. Step on up. I pull open the door and step inside. It's bobsled time.

There're only two customers in front of me (Ploughman's/Club). They're both in their seventies. Crowd control won't be a problem. Old people are terrified of Sith lords. Apparently, Darth Vader's helmet is based off trench armour worn by German soldiers during World War 1. I still won't go for the vault though. Stick to the plan. They're being served by Dracula (Chorizo/Tomato) and The Wicked Witch of The West (Coronation Chicken). I hate Coronation Chicken. Then, there she is. I haven't seen her since that last day when I showed her the win her back tattoo and she'd. No! I swallow the memory. There she is, Pesto Chi . . .

Bratwurst and Sauerkraut? What. The. Fuck? She has a new favourite sandwich? A fucking *German* sandwich? The butterflies in my stomach evolve into piranhas. Fucking Darwin! I'd introduced her to pesto. She'd said it was the best thing she'd ever tasted. She'd said she could eat it every day for the rest of her life. She'd said she'd never get sick of it. But then, she'd said a lot of things, hadn't she? She liked German saus- NO! German sandwiches now.

In my spasmatic turmoil, I squish the banana. It smears into the inside of my jumper. Damn it Zesty! I barely have time for a soul tremor before she spots me. She looks me right in the eye. She smiles. She recognises me. Of course she does. I knew she would. God in heaven help me, I can feel my traitorous face moving under the mask to return the smile. She comes out from behind the counter. Is she wearing lederhosen? She's walking over. And then she's right there. Right in front of me. She's wearing one of those Oktoberfest barmaids' costumes. Even through the mask and the smelly banana, I can smell her perfume. I've smelt it since the last time I'd seen her. There are only about a dozen perfumes women wear after all. Each time I'd freeze in place and look about sniffing the air like a startled puppy before seeing some random woman minding her own business, at which point I'd melt into a puddle on the floor. She's asking me something. Focus! At first, I don't understand. Her tone is strange. She asks again,

"Well, who are you supposed to be?"

Wait! She didn't think ... It wasn't possible. Anything but that. She didn't think I was a kid out trick or treating? But I'm taller than her! When she wasn't wearing heels. Why is she wearing heels? She'd stopped wearing them when we got together. This is a new low. How could there possibly be a new low? It's impossible. I can't move. Paralysed from the self-loathing down, I try to scream, "I'm a Darth Vader Buffalo Soldier of Fortune", but not so much as a Jamaican squeak comes out.

"Awe, are you shy?"

I've forgotten how to breathe. She picks up some monkey nuts, a pink plastic piggy bank and a Junior Super Savers Club application form and drops them in my loot satchel. I want to curl up in a ball. Only my fury saves me. That's my loot satchel! It's not a fucking monkey nut sack. But I still haven't moved an inch. She looks down at me pityingly, ruffles my hair and says

"You're a very cool robot."

Robot? I remember how to breathe, but now I'm choking on my own rage. Then, she's walking away. If I wasn't wearing the banana, I would have tried to shoot her with it. I love her and want to shoot her. I hate her and would take the banana bullet for her.

59

I'm back in the street somehow. This couldn't be further from bob-sled time. How had she not known me? I'd know her anywhere. I could identify her elbows in a police line-up. I could pick her toes out in a cannibal's freezer. And how had she thought Darth Vader was a robot? I'd made her watch *Star Wars*. She'd said she'd liked it. Said she'd liked the laser swords. It was adorable. Had she forgotten me as absolutely as she'd clearly forgotten Germany's war crimes? I should have made her watch *Schlinder's List* instead. I feel sick and exhausted. The sweaty wet suit and smell of putrid banana isn't helping. I get halfway across the bridge before I vomit most of my soul over the rail. When I'm finished heaving and blinking the tears out of my eyes, I see two swans having a splish-splash just below me a few feet away. Even if Starsky, Hutch, Robocop and John McClain had been chasing me, it still would have taken a bulldozer to get me over that rail.

I watch the swans swim through my stomach contents. Disgusting beasts. Autopilot brings me home. My first and second trick or treaters (Cheddar, Nutella) get Bob Marley's Greatest Hits on cassette and the *Cool Runnings* video. They clearly have no idea what they are. The third (Easy Singles) gets a half empty box of Rice Krispies. The fourth (Ham/cheese) is handed a pumpkin with a face carved on it that looks suspiciously like Hitler if he'd been stabbed in the face a dozen times. The fifth kid (Bananas) has a soggy wet suit flung at him. After that, I lock the door, chase Rooster into the bathroom and turn off the lights.

I cling to my tea filled hot water bottle in the dark. By the streetlight coming through the window, I see Vader looking up at me accusingly. A dickhead Sith lord is much less sympathetic than Pop. I try to blame Zesty and her funky bananas, but after weeks of kidding myself, I'm fresh out of bullshit. How did some people cocoon themselves against reality their whole lives? Surely, it's a better way to live, isn't it? To always be right and brilliant and attribute people thinking you're a dickhead down to jealousy. Ignorance must be bliss.

I think back to her birthday. I'd known she was cooling towards me. Of course I did. It was horrible, but if I made huge efforts, I could still impress her now and then. This appealed to two cornerstones of what I am, an irredeemable idiot and a kooky moron obsessed with quirky side projects. I would have enjoyed them if they weren't so desperately contrived, like a man trying to keep a sinking boat afloat with a leaky bucket. For her birthday, I emptied the wardrobe and painted her a scene from Narnia on the back panel. It was the scene of Edmund becoming corrupted by bewitched Turkish Delight from The White Witch.

We had sex that night for the first time in ages. With the lights off. It was always with the lights off by then. I tried not to take it personally that she'd started using lubricant and had swapped out the sexy red light bulb for a sensible energy saver so she could read in bed. In the morning, I woke up to her screaming. She was furious. And blue. So was I. We both had blue crotches. Like Smurfs. It was everywhere. In the dark, I'd reached for the paint instead of the lubricant. First, she ranted. Then she raved. I remember asking myself, how could the girl of my dreams not think this was hilarious? But I'd quickly swallowed the thought.

Back in the now, Rooster struts into the living room and stands in front of me, dragging me out of my shit memories.

"What are you looking at?" I ask him, but he just stands there glaring at me.

"I was never going to rob that bank, was I?"

Either Rooster shakes his head or I'm legitimately losing the plot.

"Was I the only one convinced? She's not my Pesto Chick anymore. She likes Bavarian … cuisine now. That German guy more than likely, probably doesn't have any direct connection to The Third Reich that could be proven in international court. Oh Rooster! I'd really felt like I was onto something, that I'd turned a corner. I tried to think my way out of being miserable. I'm not very clever though, am I?"

Rooster turns around and struts back out. Being occasionally self-aware can be *really* tough when you're not a janitorial ninja Keyser Söze mixed with Tyler Durden mad scientist former Mafia boss Russian spy Jamaican bob-sledding Darth Vader Scuba Raider Buffalo Soldier of Fortune.

What Other People Do

I spend the weekend in bed tormenting myself. How has everyone else managed to get the hang of being alive except me? I draw a blank.

Too Much Time on Your Hands

This is a common dig. It's a lot more common when I'm about. I'm constantly being derided for having too much time on my hands. People say it flippantly like they're not obliterating your entire existence.

And what exactly do I do with that? It's hardly constructive criticism. Nobody who does absolutely nothing has ever been accused of having too much time on their hands. It's exclusively reserved for weirdos who are doing something and that something is found to be a complete waste of time. It's an utter mystery to me what everyone else is constantly doing with themselves that's so worthwhile. I have no idea. Before I lose the last of my delusion powered momentum, I put my metaphorical trousers back on and decide to find out.

MONDAY

I call Bangers up on the telephone.

"What's wrong?" He asks.

"What? Why would something be wrong?"

"Never mind. What's up?"

"Nothing. What are you doing?"

Bangers ignores my question and instead asks "Do you want to go out or something?"

"No. What are you doing right now?"

"I was thinking about going to play some pool and maybe some poker but if you wanna do somethi-"

"Who were you going with?"

"I was gonna go by myself but if y-"

That's a relief. Bangers associates with some real savages. "Can I come?"

"To play pool? Or poker?"

"Either. Both."

"You?" The surprise in his voice leads me to suspect that, I may, in fact, be the fun police.

"Yes."

"You'd hate it."

"If I do, I'll keep it to myself. Fair enough?"

"Fair enough."

I hate it. A pool table is basically a magnet for creeps and villains. The den had the decor of a primary school sports hall, but there were more people in track suits. All the windows were tinted so the mole people would never know if they were missing a glorious day outside. We get a pool table and I'm about to take my first go when Bangers sagely says,

"If you don't chalk your cue, you've already made your first mistake."

He seems to take a strange pride in imparting this bit of wisdom. Bangers has pitch black curly hair and a little pointy beard. As soon as you're not looking at him, you can't help but picture him with cloven hooves like the devil. Or a sexually charged Mr Tumnus. He's the loosest cannon in my rogues' gallery of weirdos. A butterfly in the Amazon flaps its' wings and across the Atlantic Ocean, Bangers opens his mouth and says something that'll permanently stain the face of civilised society. His confidence is as boundless as it is baseless. We went on a lad's holiday once to Costa

Del Satan's Balls. Bangers had worked in a hostel in Costa Rica for a couple of months while backpacking around South America so we thought the fluent Spanish he assured us he spoke would come in handy. We were in a fast-food place, and he instantly took charge at the counter. With characteristic confidence, he says,

"Olá everyone! Dos cheeseburgers por favor. Ketchup solo." He then turned to us and confided, "That means two cheeseburgers just with ketchup." before looking back to the kid on the counter, "Oh! And chips please." We'd have been absolutely lost without him.

We smash the pool balls about the table for a while. More would fall in the holes if we were trying to keep them on the table. Bangers is surprisingly rubbish.

"You do this often?" I ask him.

"Maybe a couple of times a month."

"You're nearly as terrible as me. And this place is a bit bleak, no?"

"Ignore the place. Concentrate on the table. It's like one of those miniature Zen gardens. I like the levelness of the table, the smoothness of the cues, the chalkiness of the chalk, the gleam of the balls, the clack of the collision. I like to watch them collide. It's like I introduce chaos into order and get to see the effects I cause. It's like a smashy meditation."

"That's almost beautiful. If there weren't half a dozen crack heads in Burberry with tattoos on their necks sucking meat from chicken wings before throwing the bones on the floor over there, I'd be fucking moved. Are you still seeing that girl with the one smelly armpit?"

Bangers is shockingly the closest thing we have to a lady's man. We'd heard somewhere when we were kids something about how if you proposition a hundred girls, ninety-nine might say no, but one will always say yes. The rest of us had shuddered at the notion of so much rejection. Bangers had looked excited like it was some sort of mathematical guarantee of hand jobs. He's been playing the numbers game ever since.

"No, we're finished." Bangers says with real regret in his voice.

"How come?"

"We're not compatible." This is more vulnerability than you generally get from Bangers.

"Oh?"

"Sexually."

"Oh." Never mind.

"I don't expect a girl to memorise the Karma Sutra or anything, but I don't think a little bit of audience participation is too much to ask either."

"Fair enough." I say.

Bangers bends over the table and takes his shot. "Anyway, I'm caught up in this whole online business at the minute."

"Yeah? What's that like?"

He misses and pots the white ball. "I was out with some lady the other night. As in a proper lady. I should have known she was older than in her pictures. They were all in black and white. Plus, in the one of her in Pisa, the tower wasn't leaning yet. In her blurb thing, she said she likes going to 'disco concerts'. In hindsight, it's pretty obvious something was amiss. Don't get me wrong. She was a handsome woman."

I chalk my cue. If you don't chalk your cue, you've already made your first mistake. "What does that mean?"

"That's what you call a woman when she's too old to be pretty."

"Did you go back to her bungalow?"

"Even I have my limits."

"You understand that when I'm telling people this, you will absolutely have gone back to her bungalow?"

"Sure, what choice do you have? At least tell them I desecrated her like Howard Carter did the tomb of Tutankhamun in 1922."

"Pretty obscure reference mate?"

"It was one of the most significant archaeological finds ever."

"OK." And it's my turn to pot the white ball.

An hour later, we head to the back room. The difference between the idea of playing poker and the reality of playing poker is akin to the difference between a poster of a Big Mac and the sad squashed thing they throw at you in the shop. The back room is even dingier than the main hall. There isn't an international businessman or a supermodel in a cocktail dress to be seen. There's a dozen sketchy looking dudes setting up a couple of tables with cards and plastic chips. They even have green felt tablecloths. An old guy (Spam & Mustard) follows us in. He has gold teeth and a pimp cane with a gold snake's head on top. This was a huge mistake. Both he and Bangers are welcomed warmly. These guys all seem to know each other.

Trying to take money from your friends strikes me as a bit unseemly. And that's coming from a man who accidentally held an illegal cock fight in his flat immediately before pissing in a ladies' sink. Two of them (Tuna & Sweetcorn/Ham Hock Salad) are wearing sunglasses. Indoors. At night-time, so as not to reveal their "tells". I've always suspected card games were a crutch for people who can't have a proper conversation. That's why magicians are so incredibly dull. I'm sure David Blaine was making peoples' wills to live vanish long before he disappeared that elephant or whatever it was he did.

One of them (Pot Noodle) starts explaining the rules, but everyone else already knows them and I'm not paying attention. I'm way too pretentious to take instruction from someone who eats pot noodle sandwiches. It seems to me that if we still had tails, life would be a lot easier. It's impossible to bluff or play it cool with a waggy tail. You know where you stand with a waggy tail. Everyone seems OK but the conversation is pretty dismal. These James Bond wannabes are all fart jokes and sexual innuendo.

Ripping The Piss

"If you have nothing nice to say, say nothing at all." - Boring People

"If you have nothing funny to say, shut the fuck up." - Everyone I Know

Where I come from, we don't play chess or fence with rapiers. Ripping the piss is like a verbal amalgamation of both, except you must never, ever say "touché" or "check mate". It should be an Olympic sport or there should be a Nobel Prize in insults. It's complicated and nuanced. It takes years to master. You walk a tight rope of taunts. You want to be as horrible as possible just short of burning all your bridges and becoming a social pariah. When done with finesse, there's no need for any other social activity. You'll be judged on swiftness, wittiness and originality. You can say deeply cruel things as long as they're proportionally funny. Your target should be too impressed by the calibre of your mockery to be offended. And if it isn't true, you can say anything. I'll call any girl a fridge shaped, uni-browed, moustachioed, swamp monster unless it's true. If it is true, it has to be funnier than it is hurtful. It'd be pretty ambitious though to try and make an actual fat girl laugh after calling her a fridge and trying to stick a magnet to her face.

68

And for Christ's sake, never ruin some good abuse by tacking on an unnecessary "Just kidding" at the end. It undermines the whole endeavour. In some circles, you can tell how much people mean to each other by the quality of horrible things they say to each other. You'll spend more time crafting exquisite abuse for loved ones than enemies. Admissions of affection are strictly for emergencies and death beds only. This is just one of a thousand things that make us incompatible with Americans.

These gamblers cannot rip the piss. The conversation mostly revolves around how much sex they're all having with each other's mothers. It reminds me of the school yard when I was twelve.

It turns out the only skill involved in playing poker is patience. The cards are random, so the last one to surrender to boredom and declare "I'm all in bitches!" basically wins. The way these guys go on though, you'd think I was sitting around a table with Rain Man, Good Will Hunting and the bloody Horse Whisperer. I was "All in bitches!" on the third hand. I didn't even have a pair of anything.

Tuesday

I ring Marmalade.

"What's wrong?" She asks, clearly surprised to be hearing from me.

"Why would something be wrong?"

"When was the last time you actually called me on the actual phone?"

"Never mind that. What are you doing?"

"Nothing tonight. I'm already in my jim-jams."

"Fucking jim-jams? I blurt. "It's seven o'clock." You have a better chance of spotting the Loch Ness Monster giving big foot a lift than seeing Marmalade midweek. When she doesn't answer, I hazard, "Fancy some company?"

"Erm, I'm just gonna watch some telly and eat oven chips."

"Perfect. I'll see you shortly." I hang up before she can tell me to fuck off. She has Snoopy pyjamas on, and she makes me a tankard of tea.

"Do you want to watch a film or something?"

"What were you going to watch before I rang?"

"You'll hate it."

"I'm sure I won't."

I hate it, but I manage to keep my mouth shut. The difference between a man's flat and woman's is jarring. Her place is clean. It's so fucking clean. There's potpourri and pillows everywhere. You have to remove pillows from the sofa before you can sit on it. We watch a programme about people cooking food we weren't going to eat. Then, we watch a show that was just a camera following disgusting people we wouldn't want to spend time with in real life. When that finished, we watch a programme showing people sitting about watching the shows we'd just sat about and watched. It's a real effort to keep my mouth shut about Marmalade's life choices.

"Is this what you get up to during the week then?" I ask.

"Yeah, I have to get up at seven for work and I don't like to be tired, so I keep it quiet during the week."

I'm not brilliant at maths, but if she works Monday – Friday and has a strict policy of not being open to fun Sunday through Thursday night, that means that fun is only possible 2/7ths of her life which is 28.6% of the time. She hates Mondays. Wednesdays are a hump day, and she complains after Christmas that she has nothing to look forward to for eleven months. But no one ever accuses Marmalade of having too much time on her hands. There's no answers for me here.

Wednesday

Brie cancels on me Wednesday night. I put on my jacket and go to the park and sit under the moon. I compare myself to Neil Armstrong, Gandhi and Stephen Hawking. Neil? Lance? Anyway, I don't come out of this well. I think about the moon. Wilbur and Orville Wright flew a creaky plane across a field in 1903 and 66 years later, one of the Armstrongs walked on the Moon. I think about this all the time. The moon is tidally locked with us, so we always see the same side of it. It doesn't have tectonic plates like the Earth does, so apart from the very occasional meteor impact and some minor shrinkage, it's face doesn't change. Cavemen must have seen the same face when they looked up at the moon that we do. The dinosaurs must have seen it too. Apparently, the moon is drifting away from us by a couple of inches per year. If the Earth can't even hold onto the moon … I think about the old lady from the hospital. I wonder if she can stand blackberry jam since her husband died and if she can't, what can she stand? There can't be too much that doesn't remind her of him after all those years. Those blackberry jam lovers were still at it after 66 years. The Pesto Chick was too capricious for that kind of commitment.

I got home from work once to find the place covered in candles and my Pesto Chick wearing a little black frilly thing. I couldn't believe it. She hadn't done anything like this in ages. I was surprised and delighted. She homed in on my surprise like a fucking sparrow hawk. She was fiery.

"You forgot!"

"Forgot what?"

"Our anniversary." She spat. This effort wasn't for me. It was for the fucking Gregorian Calendar.

"Oh! Sorry. I hadn't even realised it was February yet. This is

71

wonderful though." I said trying to keep things light.

"'Oh? Sorry?' Is that it? I've been planning this evening for days. I swapped days off and everything."

"In secret?"

"It's our anniversary." She said through clenched teeth. I could see the tendons in her neck.

"And?"

"And I wanted to check you'd remember it. You clearly haven't."

"So, instead of us having a nice anniversary, I'm being secretly tested on my awareness of the date? Does that not strike you as a tad sadistic?"

"That's how anniversaries work. That's how everyone does it."

"Are we everyone now?" I'd asked.

"It would be nice to drink out of a cup and not have to run away every time you see a swan. What exactly are you doing with your life?"

"What?" Anniversaries are rubbish.

"You can't daydream for the rest of your life."

"You work in a sex toy shop." Actually, I'd loved how random it was that she worked in a sex toy shop, but it was my turn to say something.

"I'm gonna do an accountancy course."

"What?"

"I want more from life. You could do one too."

"I'd probably be a brilliant coal miner too, but that's another dark hole I don't want to spend my life down."

At this point, she'd started shouting at me. She'd explode while I'd implode. She was fiery. I was cool. She'd blow up into a rage when she was angry, and I'd freeze up like an unoiled Tinman left out in the rain. It wasn't pleasant having her scream in my face, but she can't have much enjoyed my Amish shunning silent treatment either. My coolness was no less involuntary than her temper though. Shouting accusations about how she was coming to despise me at her just felt futile. Can you really blame someone for being sick of the sight of you? Is it their fault?

I'd failed the anniversary booby trap, so I wanted to nail Valentine's Day. The day before, I'd ordered flowers that would arrive at the sex toy shop the next morning but that night, we got to talking about Valentine's Day presents.

"The whole dozen roses thing is such a cliché and a waste of money. Zero thought goes into it, and like, they're already dead. It's like decapitating a puppy before giving it to someone and asking if they wanna go and play fetch with it. Like, I'd much rather have a surprise pizza sent to me." She was really unsentimental.

"I completely agree."

The next morning, before she woke up, I snuck to the furthest corner of the room that the land line would stretch to and left a whispered voicemail cancelling the flowers. When I turned round, she was sitting up in bed watching me. She didn't even have the decency to pretend to be asleep. I bought my first portable telephone the next day.

Thursday

On Thursday, it's Spaghetti Hoops who calls me. We don't see each other very often. He's too tight to spend the time. We never really invite him anywhere anymore. If there's one thing I can't stand, it's tightness. If there's two things I can't stand, it's tightness and Hoops' girlfriend.

"I hear you've re-joined the living?" he says. Who the fuck told him that?

73

"Yeah. Just about. I've had a lot on."

"How are your pizza levels?" There's only one response to this question.

"Dangerously low."

"I know a great place. I'll collect you. 7 o'clock?"

"Who's going?" I ask suspiciously. I'm not going anywhere with his girlfriend (Tahini Jackfruit).

"Just me and you."

"OK. See you later."

Hoops is one of those friends who you're friends with mostly because you've always been friends. He wasn't on my list but, you know, pizza. He's freakishly tall. We were in the middle of the crowd at a music festival once, and we overheard a group of girls agree to "Meet up by the giant with the shit haircut". As well as being a giant, he has a shit haircut.

He brings me to a fucking all you can eat buffet. I heard once that if you overfeed a goldfish, it'll eat until it dies. I'm not sure why I think of this as we're seated. All around the world, plates are pretty much the same size no matter what you're eating. That's because there's a pretty much universal quantity of food that a human being should be eating. When was the last time you ate a plate of food and were still hungry? I'm not entirely sure that all the feeders here are actually land mammals. And no, none of this is glandular. Christ! There's children here. They're being allowed to eat until they're unwell. And obese. There should be a lot less stigma around just letting wolves raise your kids. In a lot of cases, they'd be better off. They'd definitely get more exercise. I don't like to think myself a judgemental person, but I will assess the fuck out of you.

Hoops tells me this is his favourite restaurant. The fucker loves a bargain, and he wouldn't give you a slide if he owned

Switzerland. Even when we were kids, the only board game he liked was Monopoly. What kind of kid would rather be a real estate developer than a Hungry Hungry Hippo? He never gets his round in, and worse, he's sneaky about it. He thinks no one notices. It's an insult to our intelligence, and basic powers of observation. He likes to have a good time, but he'd rather someone else pay for it. It's an incredibly ugly character trait. He always turns up to a party empty-handed.

Rocking Up Empty Handed

Rocking up to a party without a bottle of wine will save you a tenner, but it will result in everyone in attendance discussing how much of a miserable bastard you are behind your back. Spend the tenner. If you haven't got a tenner, stay at home.

For 11.99, we have two hours to try and eat the company out of business like we have a blood vendetta against the owners. They call these slots "feeding times". Like at the fucking zoo. We get our plates and I follow him on a whirlwind tour of the disgusting, lukewarm bain-maries of the world. Conditions in the primordial soup where life first began must have been similar to these bacterial Jacuzzis. There's a Polish guy cooking Indian food, a Spanish kid manning the fish and chips section, an Indian girl topping up the pizzas and pastas and a Chinese man behind the continental cuisine. They've got everything and they're doing none of it properly. This can't be what they had in mind when they came up with the idea of cultural integration. I want the Italian making my pizza to be so fresh off the plane that he still has his tan, and we struggle to navigate the language barrier.

75

Pizza

As I said at the start, there are idiots who say that death is a powerful aphrodisiac. It's not. It's really not. Lamentably, what really gets people revved up is when the other person plays hard to get. I was fundamentally incapable of this with the Pesto Chick. All she had to do was raise an eyebrow and I was like a rabid animal during mating season. The closest I ever got was the nights I'd go to a tavern for drinks with my deranged mates. I'd always pick up a pizza on the way home from a trattoria and be ravenous by the time I got sat down at the kitchen table. Pesto Chick was completely indifferent if I went out drinking with my friends but for some reason, she couldn't abide me drunkenly wolfing a pizza afterwards. I think it was because she didn't like not having my full attention. Wordlessly, she'd stand in front of the kitchen table like she was auditioning for one of those talent programmes and I was the judge. Then, for every slice I gobbled, she'd remove a piece of clothing. She wasn't playful. She didn't dance about. She wouldn't smile. She'd just stare at me, daring me. Her ambivalence towards me was fucking intoxicating. The Pesto Chick never asked. She demanded. She was ferocious. I didn't give her orgasms. She took them from me. She lit a fire in me. I could never get enough.

I've never known a confusion like it. With Pizza Levels dangerously low and the craving to consume mass quantities of absorbents after heavy drinking battling the need to pounce on her, it's the closest I've ever come to schizophrenia. My brain would twitch, and I'd get heartburn. I nearly choked to death more than once. It really messed up my relationship with pizza. And everything else.

Fortunately, the evil stuff they serve at this buffet is closer to being a regulation Frisbee than pizza. Hoops wraps a jalapeño popper and some carbonara in a naan and says with a full mouth,

"I'm really glad we did this. I really need someone to talk to."

For fucks sake!

"If you've joined the Taliban, I'm going home."

"Worse." He sounds a bit traumatised.

"You've started line dancing?"

"No, I kissed some girl. Saturday night."

The fucking scoundrel! I've got no time for infidelity on a good day, and in my current frame of mind, hearing about this dickhead not appreciating a girl who hasn't run off with a Nazi war criminal, even if she is unbearable, really rubs me the wrong way.

"How long have you been going out with The She-Wolf now?"

"Don't call her that." he protests.

"I'm the least of her worries." I have not missed this fucker.

"Two years."

"You've wasted two years of her time. Do you have any idea how many actual good guys she must have come across in the last two years? That she was closed off to making a connection with because she's been under the misguided assumption that you're not a creep?"

"Don't. I already feel terrible." he says as he puts a samosa on a slice of pizza and dunks it in chow mein. "I have to tell her."

"What?" I ask.

"Don't you think she deserves the truth?"

"Oh, she deserves much better than the truth kid. The truth is a fucking shambles."

"I can't handle the guilt." he whinges.

"Let me get this straight. You feel bad and your plan is to unburden yourself by telling her and shifting the misery onto her, completely clearing your conscience? That's pretty selfless alright. You don't think this is your weight to carry?"

"I thought honesty was the best policy?"

"What the fuck are you talking about? Not doing hand stuff with strangers behind the wheelie bins is the best policy. Do things or don't do them. Never reveal your true self."

"What? How did you know that? I only said I kissed her."

"Everything is always worse."

"I'm nothing without her." This was a common declaration from the more dramatic lads full of cheap cider when we were teenagers. This prick is too old for it.

"You don't seem like a whole lot with her."

"I'd expected a little bit of support." He complains.

"I'd expected artisanal pizza."

"Or understanding." he continues.

"I'm not confused mate. I get it. That angel deserves better."

"You don't even like her."

"I can't stand her. She's argumentative, pretentious and inexplicably uses more fucking Americanisms than every Troy, Brad and Chad at spring-break in Cancun. She starts calling tomorrow today the instant a clock strikes midnight instead of waiting until she'd slept like a normal person. My birthday was such a fucking anti-climax last year."

"Don't talk about her like that."

"Seriously? You're defending her honour now? That chivalry ship has sailed son. And you weren't on it."

"Next time I'll keep my mouth shut."

"Yeah do. It'll keep randomers from sticking their tongues down your throat."

He storms off but only as far as the Chinese counter. He's going nowhere while he's got another hour of eating ahead of him. He comes back with a schnitzel on top of chop suey with a side of garlic bread. Thank God the guilt hasn't ruined his appetite.

"Seriously, what do you think I should do?"

"I think you have two options. Say nothing and use the shame to fuel doing a more convincing impression of a decent human being, or tell her you're only attracted to dolphins and break up with her."

Piling pasta salad on top of a prawn cracker and launching it in the general direction of his gaping maw he says,

"Monotony is hard work."

"*Monogamy.*" I correct.

"What?"

"Monogamy is hard work."

"Yeah. What did I say?"

"Never mind."

"I love her."

Jesus! I hope he chokes on a cloud, the massive fucker.

The I Love You

The "I love you." is one of the most nebulous statements uttered in English. It can be said with complete sincerity and mean a hundred things.

It could mean "I love you. You're my all-time favourite person." Or it could mean "I love you. My happiness is entwined with yours." Or it could me "I love you. If I can't have the person I really want, I'm glad you're here." It's no wonder it leads to such confusion. And devastation.

"Aren't you going to finish that?" Hoops asks, nodding at my uneaten second plate of food. "There's starving children in Africa, you know."

"I do know. They're starving because fat, Western fuckers like us have all the food. And me finishing this won't help any of them."

"I just feel so guilty."

"About the starving children or being a dirtbag?"

"The second one."

"You never know. Maybe she's out doing hand stuff behind the wheelie bins with some random dude right now."

"Wouldn't that be ironic?"

"Actually, no."

Friday

Philly Cheese Steak and Banana Honey were sure to be home on Friday night. They've just had their second kid and I arrange to pop by and meet it. They've been together since we were all in our early twenties. I've not seen much of them since they had the first one a couple of years ago, but a friendship is like keeping a cactus. It's not much work as long as you piss on it every now and then. Plus, people really seem to appreciate it when you make the effort to meet their babies.

Their house looks like a tornado passed through and they both look exhausted but satisfied. The toddler is amusing herself on the living room floor by playing with random household objects and completely ignoring the dozens of expensive toys littering the place. There's no sign of the new one yet. I can't remember either of their names and they're too young to have sandwiches.

"Thanks for coming by." Banana Honey says as we all sit down to watch the toddler's antics.

"Of course. I should have come sooner really. I've had a lot on."

"Really?" She doesn't sound convinced.

"How are you getting on with the new guy?" I say before there's questions.

"The new guy?" Philly says confused before realisation dawns on his face "You mean our son?"

"Yeah."

"Good, thank you. What? Were you worried our personalities would clash?"

"What do we really know about this guy? You've basically let a stranger into your house."

"He should be waking up from his nap. I'll get him and you can meet him." Philly says.

"If he's asleep, don't wake him on my account."

"This is happening." Philly Cheese says decidedly. He disappears.

"Are you guys getting any sleep?" I ask Honey.

"It's not so bad. It's been crazy but amazing. They get so big so fast though. Time needs to slow down." This is something you hear from new parents all the time. Watching a tiny baby sprout up before your very eyes must make time feel like it's racing past. Philly comes back with said baby. Thank God it's not one of those unfortunate looking ones. The baby is unceremoniously flung into my arms. This is dangerously irresponsible. I take special care to support his neck as he tries to hold up his big baby head.

"Do you want oven gloves?" Philly asks.

"What? Why?" I ask, startled.

"You're holding him like he's on fire."

"Ah! Ha!"

Philly picks up the toddler and asks her "NumNumOnjieBonjie?" The kid giggles madly and they leave the room.

"What did he just say?" I ask Honey.

"Oh! He asked, 'Would you like a nice piece of orange darling?'"

"Oh?"

"And she said 'Daddy, I'd love some. Thank you.'"

"Oh! Gotcha."

"You need to get out there and meet someone."

"I did that. It was a disaster." I tell her matter-of-factly, though my stomach turns at the thought of it.

"You know, even swamp monsters and people who wear track suit bottoms and woolly jumpers find *someone*."

"Yes. That hasn't escaped my notice. Thank you. I've resigned myself to a life of bachelorhood. I'm gonna get eccentric as fuck."

"*Gonna* get?"

"Well…"

"I really do think you've got a lot of love to give. If begrudgingly." Honey says.

"What are you two talking about?" asks Philly as they come back in.

"We're trying to decide if dying alone is a good plan." Honey says.

Philly is saying something smug but in a well-meaning kind of way. I'm not really listening. I try to keep spending time with friends who have their lives together to an absolute minimum. Any nonsense self-help guru will tell you of the folly of comparing your life to other peoples' but the only other way of making an assessment would be to start keeping track of how many times you see stuff as sand through an hourglass sparking panic attacks. Thank God I don't like eggs. I wonder if they'll still have each other in sixty years. I hope they do. But yeah, it's much easier passing time with savages who still use t-shirts for pillowcases and steal all their toilet paper from pubs.

Before I know what's happening, they both disappear with the toddler leaving me with this tiny baby. These people are beyond reckless. I don't even know the baby Heimlich manoeuvre.

I inspect the little guy properly for the first time. He is pretty cute. It even feels good holding his weight in my arms, but I'm chalking that one up entirely to hard-wired biology. He locks eyes with me. Apparently, just as soon as the world cooled down enough to no longer be a molten rock fireball, life started. 3.6 billion years ago, life sparked. Just as soon as it possibly could and just once. An unbroken chain has passed through geological time for billions of years to get to us. We're the sum total of every single generation before us, managing to pair up and create the next generation. There's never been an ancestor of mine too repulsive or repulsed by intimacy who failed to extend the line. I'm the end point of a chain that goes back to that first cell dividing in two. Do I really want to be the one to break this chain that goes back to the beginning of time? I look this little chubby monster in the eye, and he vomits on me. What the fuck are they feeding him? I'm beginning to suspect that what other people do mightn't hold any answers for me.

When I get home, I pick up the phone. I've saved Beetroot for Saturday. I'm one ring from hanging up when he eventually answers the phone.

"Hello?"

"Hey pal." I say.

"Oh hello." Absolutely everyone has been surprised to hear from me.

"What are you doing tomorrow?"

"Tomorrow? I'm going to the beach."

"Do you fancy some company?"

"Sure. You can help me dig the holes. I was thinking about going pretty early?"

"I'm up at the crack of dawn these days myself." I tell him.

"Oh! OK. Why don't you call round whenever you're ready?

Don't use the doorbell. Pull the string."

"Yeah? Alright."

"OK, but I'm batman. You're Robin." And with that, he hangs up. He's been saying that to me for twenty years and it still makes me smile every time.

Saturday

Beetroot is like a constantly startled deer. No matter how nice I am to him, I always feel like I'm bullying him. It's impossible to know if he enjoys my company or he's just so polite, he's been tolerating me for two decades. He has the constitution of a lady of leisure in an eighteenth-century romance novel. He's an honest to God fainter. He was reading *1984* on the bus one time and when Winston Smith was brought into Room 101, he passed out and fell out of his seat. Another time, he invited a girl over to Netflix and Chill.

Netflix and Chill

From what I gather, young people arrange sex appointments where one will go to the other's house, and they'll silently watch reality television until they fornicate out of boredom without even having the decency to ply each other with booze and talk drivel for three hours first. It has all the charm of dogging without the nice drive in the countryside or the fresh air.

Anyway, the girl came over and they started watching a horror film in the hopes that she'd get scared and nestle into him. Long before she got spooked, there was a jump scare and Beetroot was once again on the floor. I think they decided to just be friends. He had loads of exams done. He was hoping it was a medical condition that was causing him to pass out. Turns out it's a

84

psychological thing and he's definitely a fainter. Fainting is much worse than passing out. Words are very important.

I get to his place around 9. There's a string hanging down the side of his house with a little sticker on it that says, "PULL ME". His doorbell must be broken. I shrug and give it a good yank. I hear a yowl from upstairs.

"Aaahhh! You nearly pulled my big toe off!" He yells through the upstairs window. He never disappoints. After he lets me in, he says "God, it's the crack of dawn. I wasn't expecting you 'til noon."

"I did say I was an early riser these days."

"But you're a great sleeper?"

"I'm living with a rooster now."

"Literally?"

"Literally." I confirm.

"I hate to lose you to the light side. These morning people are very judgemental of us night folk sleeping in. Where are these primitives with body clocks like farmyard animals while I'm up until five in the morning doing the important work of pondering the big questions?

"Such as?"

"Like, what if Jack The Ripper, Genghis Khan and Grace Jones were stranded on a tropical island together but they couldn't murder each other because Grace was the only one who could fish, Genghis was the only one who could make fire and Jack was the only one not too afraid of heights to climb trees for coconuts?"

"I don't know if Grace Jones is as dangerous as Jack the Ripper or Genghis Khan."

"Would you want to be trapped on an island with her?"

"Fair point."

"They actually think sleeping is a waste of time, these people. No imagination. I dreamt last night that I was a sentient beam of

85

light travelling along a fibre optic cable at the speed of light towards a prism where my consciousness would fracture to encompass the entire spectrum."

"Jesus! Then what happened?"

"I don't know. Some hooligan nearly pulled my big toe off and I woke up." he says with a smile. He's pathologically incapable of being even playfully harsh.

We get in Beetroot's ancient van. It definitely predates airbag technology. And air fresheners. The van really needs a hoover. I could tell you exactly what Beetroot had for lunch every day for the last six months. Getting in a motor vehicle with Beetroot behind the wheel doesn't require courage. Courage wouldn't be enough. You have to surrender to almost certain death. A great serenity comes over me whenever I go anywhere with him. It's like accepting your inevitable demise and finding peace with it.

With one hand white knuckled holding the roof handle and the other white knuckled braced against the dashboard, we head to the beach with Beetroot maintaining eye contact with me every time he speaks the whole way. The road is insanely winding and hilly. It's got those little, abrupt hills where you nearly leave your seat as you come down the other side, causing a tingling sensation in your nethers. It's a legitimate physiological phenomenon known as "Fizzy Willie".

Driving is a funny thing. If you're not a brain surgeon or an air traffic controller, it's the greatest responsibility you'll ever have but because it's such an everyday part of life and they'll let even the worst idiot do it, nobody thinks twice. You're basically aiming a giant bullet about town. Beetroot shouldn't even be allowed a BMX.

We arrive in one piece. The back of the van is packed with random stuff. First, we fly a kite which is strangely satisfying apart from "Let's Go Fly a Kite" from *Mary Poppins* bouncing off the inside of my skull like a rubber ball the entire time. Then, we get out a metal detector and search for treasure up and down the strand.

"How often do you do this?" I ask him.

"Usually every second Saturday."

"Have you ever found anything good?"

"I found an old broach once."

"Wow! Celtic? Norman? Roman?"

"Argos."

"Oh!"

We find a Coke can with a promotion on the side for the 1994 World Cup but that's about it. Next Beetroot produces two fishing rods.

"Do you have worms or lures or something?"

"Nah."

"Nah?"

"Do you eat fish?"

"No."

"Me neither."

"Then what are we doing here?"

"A grown man needs a pretence to be out in nature or he looks suspicious."

"Oh!"

We stand with our feet in the water and basically point sticks accusingly at the sea until our toes go numb. Then, we put our shoes back on and amble through the dunes and into the forest. We find a beautiful, old, gnarled oak tree and without a word, we begin to climb. As we sit in the tree, I say "This is great."

"Why do you sound so surprised? You've climbed hundreds of trees."

"Not for twenty years."

"All the things that were brilliant when we were kids are still brilliant now."

We sit there quietly for a while looking out to sea. Out of nowhere, Beetroot says "I like to think about a fictional altitude where all the lost balloons congregate above the clouds."

"Cool. I think about the moon."

"Yeah, the moon's good."

We sit there in silence for a long time. I get the feeling he's waiting. I resist, but this zen weirdo looks prepared to wait until the tree falls over. Eventually, I snap and blurt it all out. I tell him about the old nympho lady who lost her husband and about Snap, Crackle and that fucker Pop. I tell him about how I feel I've got no time left while wasting it all anyway. I finish by telling him about the time I didn't rob a bank. He never interrupts or asks questions. When I finish, he's silent for a long time before asking "How did you feel?"

"I felt as empty as my loot satchel."

"No, not the end. How did you feel when you were learning to swim, working on your Jamaican accent, looking for the right banana?"

"Does it matter? I completely crumbled the second I saw her."

"You didn't stick the landing, that's true, but before that, how did you feel?"

"Better than I've felt in years." I say, surprised by my own words.

"There's your answer."

"It was all bullshit. I was just kidding myself."

"You're a natural born loser."

"Cheers mate"

"No. It's a compliment. Did you actually have any plans for

the money after you robbed the bank?"

"No."

"You don't need to win. You just need to be in the game. You either need to fuel that spark of madness in yourself or snuff it out. You've done neither. That's why you feel so empty all the time. There's a lot a boy has to give up to become a man. You haven't given it up yet, but you're not using it either. The only time you should drag your feet in this life is while walking through crunchy, autumn leaves. You're sitting on the metaphorical fence. Sitting on the fence isn't comfortable. You've got metaphorical splinters in your metaphorical arse."

I did! I did have metaphorical splinters in my metaphorical arse!

"People need a creative outlet." He continues.

"Not the ones I spent my week with."

"The mad ones do. You've got your side projects. That's a rare thing. Throw yourself into them."

"Which one?"

"You'll know it when you see it. You need to find something worthy of your dedication."

"Worthy of my dedication? That's a tad grandiose."

"This a big talk we're having."

"What about you? What's your creative outlet?"

"I don't need one. I'm working on inner peace."

"That sounds good."

"It's not for you."

"Why not?"

"You hate yourself too much. You need to be distracted from yourself. You need to be out there. Do you know anyone who gets in trouble like you?"

"No." I sigh.

"It's a gift. Follow your instincts."

"Anything could happen yet?"

"Exactly. There's worse things than being a loser."

"Like what?"

"Like a sore loser. Or an arrogant winner."

"You don't think I'm arrogant?"

"You don't have the confidence to be arrogant. You are occasionally obnoxious. And honestly, pretty pedantic."

"You're not the weirdo everyone thinks you are." I say.

"No, I am. It's just that you are too."

"I should have called you on Monday."

"Monday? I mucked out my rabbit hutch and did three hours of Bikram yoga."

"Never mind."

The Prodigal Flatmate

The next morning, after shutting Rooster up by throwing the collected *Chronicles of Narnia* at him, I go back to bed and am later woken by a knock at the door. I try to ignore it, but after the third round of banging, I surrender and go to see who it is. It's Hotdog. He's off the crutches but wearing stripy chinos and a lime green jumper. He's a technicolour portrait of misery.

"Hey, what's going on?" I ask.

"Can I come in?" He's looking sheepish and keeps averting his gaze like a fucking serial killer. This doesn't feel like a social call.

"Tea?"

"Yeah. Cheers."

We sit down around the kitchen table, sipping tea from a champagne flute and a Martini glass.

"You look fresh. Have you lost weight?" he asks.

"Yeah, maybe." Between all the exercise, swimming and eating the vegetables I'd had to buy from the market to appear less mental, I've lost the weight I'd found after the break-up, and I'd found quite a bit. I'd been struggling to motivate myself to do anything, so as an experiment, I started treating myself to a dessert every time I accomplished anything, and I mean *anything*. I called it Pavlov's Pavlova. It got to the point where I was leaving the house to buy pavlova just to reward myself for leaving the house. It was a vicious circle, and after a while, so was I. I'm definitely not handsome enough to get away with being a fat bastard.

"Honestly, you look five years younger." Hotdog says.

"Calm down. It's just spinach. It's not a time machine."

Hotdog deflates in his chair like he's lost all hope.

"Spill it. You're freaking me out." I say once the silence becomes too much.

"Well, the thing is" he starts.

"Woah! Hold your horses. List your three good things first."

"Oh! Erm . . .

- Raindrops on roses
- Whiskers on kittens
- Bright copper kettles and warm woolen mittens"

"OK." Wait! Is that fucker just deadpanning *The Sound of Music?* "Oi! No cheating. Try again"

"Ermmm, when I was ten, I was at the train station with my mother. There were people on the opposite platform across the tracks waiting for a train too. Then it started raining on their side. We were in the sunshine watching people fifteen feet away get rained on. They were looking back at us in the sun, absolutely raging."

"Is that true? I ask, genuinely impressed.

"Yeah."

"That'll do nicely." I roll my finger, gesturing for him to continue with his latest calamity.

"Have you seen the news?"

"No. Why?"

"Remember I told you I was gonna invest in some art?"

"Yeah?" I say cautiously.

"Well, I did. Two weeks ago. I got a good deal. I bought three paintings by a very famous didgeridoo player."

The Famous Didgeridoo Player

A very famous Australian singer, painter, children's television presenter and didgeridoo player had recently had his hard drive checked. It wasn't full of pictures of kangaroos.

"Who? . . . Oh!" My stomach drops for him. "Jesus! How much did you spend?"

"Twenty-five grand." he whispers.

"Christ!" I flinch. "How much are they worth now?"

"I could cover them in glue and stick three posters of sad clowns in the frames I suppose." he says trying his best at a sad smile.

"I suppose they don't offer insurance for that kinda thing. You're broke then?"

"Fucked." There's a heavy silence before Hotdog sighs, gets up and heads to the bathroom. He's pissing with the door open when he shouts through the wall "Mate?"

"Yes mate?"

"Why is there a chicken in the bath?"

"I'm defrosting him." I shout.

"What?" he asks as he walks back in, drying his hands on his stripy trousers.

"He's not a chicken. He's a rooster"

"Oh!" he sits back down. "But where did he come from?"

"It's a long story and I only remember half of it. I'm kinda stuck with him."

"I'll kill him for you if you like?" he offers so casually that my blood freezes.

"What? Like with a knife?" When exactly did I become attached to Rooster? I'm on the verge of a panic attack here.

"No, you idiot. I'll snap his neck." As he says this, he mimes

93

putting his two clenched fists together and making a breaking motion like how I'd snap a Toblerone. This is big talk from Hotdog. He's no more manly than I am.

"Seriously?" Doesn't it always seem to go, that you don't know what you've got until someone threatens to murder it in the bath?

"Yeah, I used to stay with my granny during the summer when I was little. She kept chickens. I'd help." Hotdog's nonchalance is spine chilling.

"Help kill chickens? How old were you?"

"First time I did it? Six or seven."

"Jesus Christ! Was she fucking Amish? Your fucking family! You stay away from Rooster."

Hotdog shrugs and stands up to look out the kitchen window onto the back yard. He looks tormented, but in an over the top, daytime soap opera kinda way. Eventually, he turns to me and says, "Look, is there any chance I could maybe move back in?"

Well, we've certainly been through a lot to get back to exactly where we started. Classic Hotdog. "Your parents driving you mental?"

"How did you guess?"

"Mate, before you moved back in with them, you phoned home less often than E.T. I assume from your butcher days, you're not allergic to feathers?"

"No?"

"OK then."

I spend the day helping Hotdog move all his stuff back in with the exception of three pervert paintings. We stop off at the site of the previous week's bonfire and put them in the centre of the scorched earth and set them ablaze. Hotdog seems to think this is some sort of exorcism. The gesture is artier than the paintings were to be honest. Looking into the devil's flames, I find the whole thing quite charming. We pick up a Chinese takeaway and a bottle of red on the way home. As we sit at the kitchen table eating noodles out of the plastic trays, using old knitting needles as chopsticks because we have no clean forks, I say to Hotdog "Open up mate."

He takes a deep breath and begins, "I just really thought this art and antiques thing was gonna be my thing. You know, the thing that sorts me out and pulls my life together. There's been leaps and bounds with the stigma surrounding depression. Which is brilliant. There's all kinds of support for them now, but just being sad all the time is fucking embarrassing. You wait for your life to change. Years go by. Everything stays the same."

Christ! And he's looking at me with haunted eyes to say something. "I meant open up the wine." I admit limply.

"Oh!" he says, clearly disappointed. Jesus! His lip is trembling. Why is his lip trembling? He passes the bottle to my side of the table, stands up and walks out. After a couple of heartbeats that I can hear in my ears, I hear his bedroom door close. The silence in the flat is thick. I like to think my friends know that they can talk to me if they need to, but I also like to think that they know this mate service should only be availed of in emergencies. I've got a sinking feeling this was one of those emergencies. I might have to make it up to him.

"For fuck's sake!" I say to my chow mein. There really isn't room for *two* sad dudes *and* a rooster in this flat. I decide I'm going to have to help Hotdog. "Fucking antiques?"

The next morning, Rooster has us both lolloping out of our rooms in our underpants at dawn. Hotdog throws a copy of GQ at him and shouts "Shut up, you fowl prick!" That obviously wasn't going to accomplish anything. Rooster is accustomed to being barraged by hefty classics from the English literary canon. He isn't

95

about to be silenced by anything with Gwyneth Paltrow on the cover. I hand Hotdog a copy of Paradise Lost which he launches at Rooster.

"Your days are numbered dickhead." he says to Rooster. Then we both retreat into our rooms without another word.

Later, I go to every antique market and charity shop in town. I even find a car boot sale. Eventually, I find what I'm looking for. The next morning, I'm up with Rooster. At nine o'clock, Hotdog hears shouting coming from my room and barges in a few seconds later in his boxer shorts to find me standing on the bed still bellowing. He notices the noise coming from somewhere that sounds like demented church bells.

"What the fuck is that?" he asks.

"It's coming from the floor." I tell him. Hotdog pulls away the rug like a prissy matador and looks at the floorboards as if they might conceal a trapdoor to hell.

"That board looks loose." I point out. "I've got a screwdriver here. Pry it up." I take the screwdriver from the shelf above my bed and hold it out for him to take.

"What? It's your room. You do it." The noise stops and it's all suddenly too quiet.

"Go on then." I insist. Hotdog hesitantly sticks the screwdriver between the floorboards and levers. The loose board pops up easily, surprising him. What Hotdog sees turns him white as a ghost. He pulls up a dusty but perfectly preserved chicken with a crucifix wrapped around its neck and an antique bone handled corkscrew screwed into its chest lying on top of an ancient looking Ouija board. Two thousand years of superstition and dogma seem to rattle Hotdog's insides. I take the Ouija board and bird and lead him into the kitchen and put the kettle on. While Hotdog drinks tea from the spout of a watering can, I point out,

96

"The bird is freezing cold. Touch it."

"No way!"

Hotdog wants to call a priest, the police and the fire brigade. In that order. And only because Ghostbusters aren't a real thing.

"Put the phone down. The Other Side wants to tell us something." I tell him.

"I thought you didn't believe in The Other Side?" he counters suddenly suspicious.

"Of course I believe in The Other Side. I'm not an idiot."

"I don't think it's a good idea."

"Let me tell you what's not a good idea. Ignoring the wishes of The Other Side. Now *that's* not a good idea."

Hotdog paces back and forth in the kitchen, rubbing his chin as he thinks, much like they used to do in old films, but no one has ever actually done in the history of stressed-out Homo sapiens. "Yeah, maybe. Should we ask Fathe-"

"No! That's another bad idea."

"OK. Should we wait until it gets dark or something?" He asks uncertainly.

"You're a terrible idea machine today."

We wait until it gets dark. I set the board up on the kitchen table while Hotdog lights some candles and Rooster pecks my ankle. I coax him into putting his hands on the planchette. He doesn't question how I randomly know the nomenclature.

"Say something." I say.

"Why me? It was in your room."

"You're the Catholic."

Seeing the sense in this, Hotdog gathers his nerve and says "Hello?"

After a moment, the planchette begins to move slowly across the board, stopping on a letter before moving onto the next.

HELLO

"Who are you?" Hotdog asks.

I'M

There is a pause.

SAINT FRANCIS OF

Another longer pause.

A ZI ZI

"A Zi Zi?" asks Hotdog confused.

YES

"OK?"

GOD IS ANGRY AT THOUGH

"Though?"

THOW

"Thow?"

THEE

"Me?"

YOU

"What have I done?"

YOU KNOW WHAT YOU ARE DOING YOU KNOW WHAT YOU ARE

"I don't. I'm not."

YOU ARE

"I'm not. I've nev-"

GOD MADE YOU TO LOVE YOUR FELLOW MAN ALL YOU DO IS HATE YOURSELF BE GAY GO FORTH KISS BOYS GOD IS COOL WITH IT

Hotdog sits there stunned. There is a brief pause before the planchette moves again.

DON'T KILL ROOSTER

There is a longer pause

DO THE FROZEN WASHING UP

The planchette stops moving. We both take our hands off it. There's a look of utter astonishment on Hotdog's face for a moment and then he bursts into tears. I sit there watching my friend cry open, unashamed tears of pure relief. He's utterly convinced. Hotdog will be OK now, I think. He can have his God and be himself. I make a decision there and then. I decide that if I can't figure out how to live a full, happy life, I'll live a charmed one. If life isn't charming, I'll make it so. That's a worthy project. Something worthy of my dedication.

It doesn't take much to convince Hotdog that we'll need to get rid of the Ouija board. I know I'll turn him into my monkey butler pretty much instantly otherwise. We go back to the site of our last ritualistic bonfire and torch the accursed board game and the semi-frozen rooster. Hotdog doesn't say anything on the walk there but as we watch the fire, he finally says, "Mate?"

"Yes mate?"

"I, em, I think I might be gay."

"Really mate?" I put all the surprise in my voice I can muster.

"Yeah." He's got tears in his eyes. It's taken him thirty-five years and a poorly planned miracle riddled with spelling errors to say that.

"That's OK mate. As long as you're happy, that's all that matters."

"I haven't been happy mate. Not at all." This poor, homophobic, religious bigot would actually break your heart.

"I know mate."

"Should we tell someone?" he asks.

"I'll report you to the authorities in the morning."

His brow creases in confusion for a second. "I mean about the Ouija board."

"It's probably best if we keep that to ourselves. The Pope will end up getting involved and coming to visit. We'd have to clean the windows and wash the curtains. Rooster'd end up pecking him."

He shakes his head from side to side as though weighing up this point.

"So, what are you gonna do now?" I ask him.

He shrugs, "Kiss boys, I guess. Where will I find them though?"

"I believe there's special discotheques for that nowadays."

"Oh yeah! Do you know any?"

"Actually, I do. It's called Gash. They do karaoke on Sundays."

"Will you come with me?" he asks nervously.

"On your great sexual odyssey? OK, but you'll have to do all the boy kissing yourself."

"Thanks. Mate?"

"Yes mate?"

"It's not too late, is it?"

"For what?"

"For us. To be happy."

"Oh, no mate. Anything could happen yet."

As the flames burn, we begin to smell the roasting rooster.

"Mate?" I say more upbeat.

"Yes mate?" He sounds more cheerful too.

"We should have a barbecue." I suggest.

"OK mate."

The Stock Room

The next day, filled with a newfound sense of optimism after my amazing result helping Hotdog and an uncharacteristic desire to help my fellow man, I head back to the charity shop where I'd picked up the Ouija board. On the way, I noticed a homeless man (Meatballs) sitting outside a shop. He's got nothing but a backpack, a sleeping bag and a paper cup. I'd seen him sitting in the same spot when I'd gone to the Ouija board. He's about my age and much less scruffy. I'm momentarily daunted by the gargantuan challenge of helping my fellow man, but I shake it off.

The charity shop is run by a beautiful, hippy lady in her early forties (Roasted Pumpkin & Goat's Cheese). Pumpkin had been very excited by my interest in the Ouija board. She recognises me,

"So, did you have any luck contacting The Other Side?"

"I had great success raising spirits." I tell her. There it is. The best thing I'll ever say, and she doesn't get it. There's no justice.

I offer to do some volunteering in the shop. This is partly due to my newfound sense of altruism but mostly because I'd gotten a brief glance of the storeroom in the back the last time I was here. My imagination has been running wild ever since, turning it into an Aladdin's cave of treasures, wonders and arcane curiosities. In many ways, getting pecked by that Swan was the worst thing that ever happened to me. It proved that there was magic in the world. There just wasn't very much of it. I've been looking for more ever since. I've found none. I did manage to fabricate some yesterday though.

I start there and then. On closer inspection, the storeroom is less an Aladdin's cave of treasures, wonders and curiosities than a tomb of litter, scrap and rubbish, but I've already accidentally committed to volunteering one afternoon a week. This is only daunting for a few minutes however. It turns out that volunteering for charity isn't nearly as rubbish as you'd instantly assume. I quite enjoy it actually. It's like working a normal job except the boss has zero leverage on me and I'm in no way obligated not to take the piss. Obviously, this means the quality of my customer service varies wildly and I come down like a Bob Geldof shaped ton of bricks on anyone trying to haggle with charity. This happens more often than you'd think. It seems people visiting charity shops are usually there more through cheapness than selflessness. The frugal are like terrorists. Never negotiate with them.

"How much are these jeans?" asks someone's austere, angry lesbian auntie (Chicken & Ham Paste) with a Vanilla Ice 1994 flat top haircut. If she's not at least an amateur darts champion in her local league, I'll eat her leather waistcoat.

"The price is on them, I think?" I know it is, but I act confused by her confusion.

"It says they're a tenner?" she says somehow turning it into a question.

"OK." I know exactly where this is going but look utterly baffled.

"I'll give you 7."

Trap sprung. "No, you fucking won't." I do a pretty good job feigning indignation that she would even suggest such a thing.

"Excuse me." Her jaw might reach the floor.

"No, I won't."

"You're very rude."

"And how would you describe someone trying to steal 3 quid of rice from the mouths of starving orphans?"

"This is a charity shop for the blind." She corrects.

"*What?* The starving orphans are blind too? Get out!"

"I'll take my business elsewhere." Is she trying to *Pretty Woman* me? She's the one who has made a big mistake. Huge!

Pretty Woman

Pretty Woman is a 1990 romantic comedy starring Julia Roberts and Richard Gere about a wealthy businessman who hires a financially vulnerable young woman to be his sexual plaything. It's Brilliant!

"Yeah, maybe you can go to the electrical shop next door and barter some socks you've knitted and a fish you caught in the river for a new hoover."

"Well, I never." Someone dressed like a long-distance truck driver from the 80s has never sounded so snooty.

"You have now. Jog on." I find charity work very rewarding.

Meatballs is still in the street when I finish volunteering. I pop into a deli and buy him a meatball sub. He's legitimately overcome with emotion when I hand it to him. His eye's instantly well up and I internally root against gravity as it tries to pull the tears from his eyes. It's no good. Fuck you Newton! Toxic masculinity kicks in pretty quick and he pulls himself together, while I pretend to check the time on a watch that I'm not wearing. When he's ready, we chat for a couple of minutes. Apart from the cold, hunger, and general insecurity of living outside like a dog where any maniac can interfere with you while you sleep, homeless people can be incredibly lonely and go days without speaking to anyone. He tells me that he's a qualified electrical engineer. It's terrible to see a grown man feel the need to justify himself to a stranger like this. I wish him well and go home to my warm flat.

Proper Preparation Prevents Pointless Parties

The change in Hotdog is sudden and bloody marvellous. The sullen, horrendously dressed man-child, out of nowhere has a spring in his step. He even seems to be getting along with Rooster. We plan the barbecue. We never had a flat warming party when we moved in as we'd both been gloomy as fuck. Hotdog is surprised when I tell him to leave the food shopping to me because I'm going to get some exotic meats.

"What do you mean, exotic meats?" He asks with furrowed eyebrows.

"Exactly that. If we're going to start entertaining, we're going to do it right. We're gonna offer an experience unlike any other."

"We are?" His voice is nearly as high pitched as a dog whistle.

"We are." I assure him. "And they'll be utterly charmed."

"Utterly charmed?"

"Utterly charmed." I shake a fist at him to emphasise how seriously we're taking this "And they'll bloody like it."

"What animals will we be eating then?" He's looking at me like he's suddenly found out he lives with a cannibal.

"I spoke to my meat guy and he sai-"

"You have a meat guy?" He interrupts baffled.

"Yes. I spoke to my meat guy, and at the moment, he has bison, camel, crocodile, flamingo, giraffe, frog's legs, kangaroo, penguin, snake, springbok, wild boar and zebra."

"What the fuck! Which one are we getting?"

"We're getting the lot. It's gonna be a Turbo Exotic Barbecue."

"Isn't November a bit late for a Turbo Exotic Barbecue?"

"It's never too late, but yes. Yes, it is. That's where you come in. While I'm out murdering the camel, it's your job to pick up a dozen hot water bottles and leis."

"What are leis?"

"Those Hawaiian flower necklace things."

"Oh! What do we need those for?"

"So, you can tie them to the hot water bottles and make hot water bottle necklaces."

"Oh!" He's biting his upper lip, clearly daunted.

"Draw Tiki faces on them or something. It'll be as tropical as a Capri Sun and there's a huge mint bush growing in the back yard. If we can keep the guests from pissing on it, we can make Mojitos."

He brightens, "This sounds like a great party. How come we never did this before?"

"Because you're a miserable fucker." I say but I give him a smirk so he knows I'm owning my part of it.

My first stop is the market and I head straight to my favourite stall. Zesty Prawn's face lights up when she sees me. "Hello. I haven't seen you here in a while?"

"Hey. Yeah, I had a banana that didn't agree with me." I tell her. Her brow wrinkles in concern.

"I'm joking. I've ha-"

"Had a lot on?"

Surprised, I raise my own eyebrow at this. "Yeah. It's a long story."

"How long?" she asks.

"105 pages." I say, breaking the fourth wall.

"I'd love to hear it." She sounds hopeful. I decide hopeful is good but then there's an awkward silence and she looks shy before continuing. "So, how many bananas can I get for you today?"

"None, thank you. I do need some limes, lettuce, tomatoes, cucumbers and a dozen pineapples."

"A dozen pineapples?"

"I'm having a Turbo Exotic Barbecue. Actually, would you like to come? It's tomorrow. I know it's a bit cold and all but we hav-"

"Yes!" she blurts before looking away and beginning to blush. It's actually very cute.

"Oh! Great." I give Zesty the address, pay for the fruit and veg and am about to leave when she asks, "Wait! What time?"

"Sundown." She looks dubious, so I just leave. Leaving without explaining things is a bit mysterious. Making plans at sunset is very mysterious. Making plans at sunset *and* not explaining things is incredibly mysterious. I go to get the meat. On the way home, I pop into the fishmongers and pick up some prawns.

The Turbo Exotic Barbecue

One of Hotdog's supermarket mates (Eggy Soldier) offers to DJ for us. He turns up with computers, gizmos and do-dads and begins setting up in the kitchen. Apparently, he has over fifty thousand songs on his floppy disks or whatever, but when I ask if he has the *Space Jam* soundtrack, he says no. I tell him I have it covered. Our only music since I gave away Bob Marley's *Greatest Hits* is a cassette of the *Space Jam* soundtrack.

Space Jam
Space Jam is a 1996 film starring Bill Murray, Michael Jordan and the Looney Tunes. It's brilliant! The soundtrack features Coolio, LL Cool J, Busta Rhymes, Aaliyah and Method Man. The biggest hit from the album was I Believe I Can Fly by a pre-disgraced R. Kelly. He never should have pissed on all those girls.

When Eggy asks what our Wi-Fi password is, he receives a blank stare and an agonising silence. A couple of weirdos with a video player in this day and age are unlikely to have the World Wide Web in their home. We don't have any blue teeth either.

Rasher and Marmalade arrive next with Rasher's sister. I haven't seen Rasher's sister since the funeral. She takes me by the hand and tells me "You're looking a million times better. I've been praying for you." I'm too embarrassed about her wasted prayers to tell her about the fake tan, so I just thank her and make a mental note to despise myself later.

"The place looks great. says Marmalade. "I love all the different coloured light bulbs."

"Ssshhhh! They aren't for the party. I put them in the other day to see if Sherlock Monochromes would notice. I've been rotating different colours into different rooms whenever he's not about." Tonight, the living room is red, the hallway is green, the stairs are blue and there's a purple light coming out of Hotdog's room.

"You're conducting experiments on your oldest friend in the world?" asks Marmalade.

She gets nothing but a deadpan, "Yes."

Exasperated, "And?"

"Inconclusive. He'll occasionally look up, confused like a springer spaniel who smells something interesting. I'll pretend not to be scrutinising him and he'll almost say something, shrug and go back to whatever he's doing. Maybe the different colours have slightly different brightness levels? I don't know. I might try dying some of his more radioactive clothes next."

"You're a real Tesla." Marmalade says.

"He's more like a Nazi scientist." Rasher corrects.

Hotdog comes over to greet our guests before taking Rasher and Marmalade aside to tell them his big news. Their surprise is about as convincing as Hotdog's heterosexuality had been, but he doesn't seem to notice. Some of Hotdog's friends from the supermarket turn up. Meat Lover comes with his new boyfriend and upon seeing Hotdog in purple leopard print instantly offers to take him shopping. Everyone loudly agrees on his behalf.

The doorbell rings and I go to let Bangers in.

"Alright?" I say.

"What's the story?"

"The other fella knows." I tell him.

"Knows what?"

"That he's gay."

"No way! Who told him?" Bangers looks at me accusingly.

108

"He figured it out."

"By himself? Wow! How did he take the news?" he whispers, "Is he afraid Jesus will cause a fuss?"

"No. I think they worked it out between them. Just pretend to be surprised when he tells you."

He chuckles while shaking his head, "I'll do my best."

"Nice one. Also, as he's coming out, we're going out."

"Out out? His eyes light up, suddenly excited.

"Out out out."

"Far out!" He's not the best at word play.

"Get out!"

"Sorry."

"Yeah. We're going to that gay club though. OK?"

"Deadly! It's wall to wall fanny in that place with girls avoiding fellas like us."

Fellas like *us*? I'm not sure how I got dragged down to his level. We walk in and he quietly says to me while surveying the room. "I thought there'd be more women here?"

"What on Earth gave you that idea?" I ask him.

"Fair enough." he says with a shrug.

The next bang on the door is Zesty.

"Hey. Thanks for coming." I say as I invite her in.

"Thanks for inviting me. I made you something." she says with hints of mischief and shyness.

"Really?"

Zesty pulls a container out of her bag and opens it. A wave of nausea comes over me and my saliva glands go into overdrive the way they only do just before you get sick. What the fuck is happening to me? I inhale again and I know what it is. I snatch the box off her and put the lid back on.

"It's banana bread." she explains while looking at me sideways.

You wouldn't think my life was interesting enough to produce PTSD flashbacks, but I'm suddenly back in the bank, sweating and being suffocated by a wet suit that's at least one size too small with the stench of that soggy banana taunting me. However, Zesty is still looking at me expectantly. I try to shake it off and compose myself as I wipe the spontaneous sweat from my brow. Then I realise what she's saying. "Wait. You actually made this? For me?"

"Yeah." she says with an implied "Duh!".

I'm disproportionately touched by the gesture. I mean, she must have measured out ingredients, mixed them, preheated an oven. Greaseproof paper will have been involved somehow. This is a quantifiable gesture. Holding it in my hands, I can feel the weight of it. I'm moments away from displaying an earnest emotion before I reign myself in. I give her my most sincere thank you.

I make sure that everyone has a hollowed-out pineapple filled with Mojito but abstain myself as Rasher's sister is watching me like a prohibition hawk. Hotdog even got those little umbrellas. I introduce everyone to Rooster and lead them out onto the deck. It's a clear, crisp night with a full moon. The yard looks amazing. Hotdog has gotten enough fairy lights and candles to safely land a plane. Our deck is huge and takes up most of the yard. The barbecue smoulders to one side. Three steps lead down to our little empire of weeds, bushes and briars. It's been at least a couple of previous tenants since anyone took an interest in gardening. Picking up two pineapples from the buffet table, I bang them together to try and get everyone's attention. This is obviously worse than useless, so I just start shouting.

"Thanks for coming everyone. I hope you're all starving. We have something special for you tonight. Let me see if I can remember everything. We have **b**ison, **c**amel, **c**rocodile, **f**lamingo, **f**rog's legs, **g**iraffe, **k**angaroo, **p**enguin, **s**nake, **s**pringbok, **w**ild boar and **z**ebra." They're all shocked and intrigued. Marmalade looks a bit horrified. I'll get them to charmed though.

Earlier, I'd marinated pork, venison, rabbit and pheasant breasts in variations of five different Turbo Exotic Sauces. Some I'd "tenderised" with a hammer. There's an illusion of a lot more variety than is the case. Who the fuck would actually eat an actual giraffe? It all goes on the grill. It all gets flipped. Pheasant is like chicken in that the instant between being afraid it might still be riddled with salmonella and it turning into cardboard can be measured in picoseconds. I'm sure penguin would be the same if we had any. As each portion is cooked, I randomly make up what animal it is and put it in a burger bun. Then I sense the perfect guest to eat it and send it their way. Who would eat a giraffe? These savages would, and as far as they know, they are. No questions asked.

I hear laughter, look over my shoulder and see Hotdog and Rasher entertaining Zesty. I can just hear Hotdog say, "And then, out of nowhere, the biggest swan you've ever seen in your life came straight for us."

"Completely unprovoked." adds Rasher.

"Yeah, completely unprovoked." Hotdog agrees.

A few seconds later everyone is laughing. I sigh and smile at the same time. The hot water bottle necklaces and rum work a treat, and everyone is happy to stay outside under the moon. I do bloody love the moon.

"Where's Rooster?" Rasher asks after he's finally stopped stuffing his face with faux flamingo long enough to come up for air and take a look around.

"What do you mean? You just ate him." I tell him. Rasher

turns green before ranting and raving at me for a solid two minutes. This is indeed a charming barbecue. I rush inside to change the music after I notice someone has put Bob Marley on. I meet Ham Hock by the stereo. Of course, it was Hock who put Bob Marley on. Bangers reckons he's the most boring man who ever lived. This is a tad unfair. He's maybe the most boring man alive today. In the English-speaking world. Having him at a party is a bit like a mean-spirited version of tag where if you get cornered talking to him, you fob him off on someone else, like an unwanted orphan on a rich lady's doorstep as quickly as possible. It's important to stay mobile. I got stuck with him earlier because I needed to stay by the grill. Eventually I shepherded him like a bored sheepdog over to Bangers who was laying low in the kitchen.

"Tell him about the time you got bitten by that Cambodian prostitute." Before Bangers could curse my name, I bolted.

"Why did we even invite him?" I ask Hotdog.

"You said it would add a sense of boring danger to the party.'"

Hotdog has an annoying habit of exactly remembering things I've said. This would be flattering if I didn't talk so much rubbish.

"He is a real sweetheart. He'd do anything for you." I say.

"He couldn't do enough for you." Hotdog agrees.

"Best in the world."

"Salt of the Earth."

"I've never heard him say a bad word about a man, woman or child." I say.

"Why would he slag off a child?" Asks Hotdog.

"We would."

"Only if it was a dick."

"He's a much better person than us." I admit.

"It's not enough."

"It's just not enough." I agree emphasising each word.

112

"He's already talked at me about professional golf for six minutes. Unbelievable." Hotdog moans.

"I had a brief update about what's happening with Formula One. It's fucking driving. He could sit in his garden and watch cars go past live. Jesus! He could jump in his car and do it himself. I've got interests that no one else cares about. I wouldn't dare bore people with them."

"You would if you thought you'd get away it."

I have no comeback to this, so I go to check on the meat.

After everyone has left except Rasher, Rasher's sister, Bangers, Marmalade and Zesty, I come outside to hear Rasher say to Zesty,

"We nearly didn't come at all."

"Why?" she asks.

"The last time he cooked, it was kind of a mess."

"It was a fucking disaster." Bangers corrects.

"That was ten years ago." I protest.

"He didn't give someone food poisoning, did he?" she asks while giving me a playful look.

"Worse." Rasher says.

"He killed someone?" she guesses again.

"Worse." says Hotdog.

"He killed two people?" Zesty is pretty funny.

"I didn't kill anyone." I say already exhausted with where this is going.

"What could be worse than killing someone?"

"It was worse." Marmalade attests.

"It was a mild gastronomic misstep." I say.

"Misstep? It was a fucking culinary calamity." Marmalade says.

"It was a bubbling cauldron of horse shit, is what it was." Bangers isn't famous for sparing feelings. Everyone agrees. I know what's coming. I'm not alone in believing that over-reacting is

113

under rated. It's kinda one of the things we all have in common. This is an old tale. They can all tell it. They tell it well. It's kind of like their party piece.

"Please don't." I plead. Rasher begins. These amateur drama society weirdos perform this like a play, so I'll write it as such. It absolutely does not merit a flashback.

The Curry

Rasher: "Gather round everyone. The Year: 2009"

Bangers: "The Location: A kitchen very much like the one just yonder."

Rasher: "Gordon Oliver here decided to cook a curry and invited us all round. He planned it for days. He picked the finest, freshest ingredients from the spice pallet of the mysterious subcontinent of India."

Hotdog: "The *freshest* ingredients"

Rasher: "The choicest cuts of free-range chicken."

Marmalade: "The *choicest.*"

Bangers: "Herbs and spices."

Rasher: "Spices and herbs."

Marmalade: "Jasmine and coriander."

Hotdog: "Turmeric and cumin."

Rasher: "He pestled and mortared."

Bangers: "He mortared and pestled."

Hotdog: "He was seasoning and basting and marinating for days."

Rasher: "We beseeched him. 'You're killing yourself' we said, but he wouldn't listen."

Hotdog: "It's not often we beseech someone."

Marmalade: "But it was all worth it. He conjured a maelstrom of colours and textures, colliding, rebounding and mixing."

Bangers: "He brought all the flavours together and balanced them like a ballet performance, no one herb or spice stepping on the toes of another."

Marmalade: "The chicken, he basted, tenderised, sautéed and

115

marinated to perfection."

Rasher: "It would melt if you gave it a stern look."

Bangers: "The aroma permeated the ether, entrancing everyone within two miles."

Marmalade: "As the crow flies."

Bangers: "As the crow flies."

Marmalade: "'Give us a taste', we implored."

Hotdog: "'Get the fuck out of my kitchen', he parried."

Rasher: "It was enough to drive you mad."

Marmalade: "The sauce was thick and . . . saucy. And oh, the rice!"

Hotdog: "Tell us about the rice."

Marmalade: "It was the fluffiest rice you'd ever seen."

Hotdog: "How fluffy was it?"

Marmalade: "It was fluffy as a cloud."

Rasher: "An altocumulus cloud?"

Marmalade: "Fluffier"

Bangers: "A stratocumulus cloud?"

Marmalade: "Fluffier"

Rasher: "A cumulus cloud?

Marmalade: "Fluffier."

Hotdog: "Not a cumulonimbus cloud?"

Marmalade: "It was fluffy as a cumulonimbus cloud."

Bangers: "That's a fluffy cloud."

Marmalade: "It was a fluffy rice."

Rasher: "And *that* was where he made his fatal mistake."

Everyone: "DUN-DUN-DUUUNNNNN"

Me: "It wasn't fatal."

Rasher: "And *that* was where he made his fatal mistake."

Everyone: "DUN-DUN-DUUUNNNNNNNNNNNNNNNNN"

Hotdog: "By the time anyone noticed, it was too late."

Marmalade: "He . . . He . . . I'm sorry. I can't."

116

Rasher puts his arm around her shoulder. Amateur drama societies have a lot to answer for.

Rasher: "It's OK. It's not your fault. I'll do it. By the time anyone noticed, it was too late."

They wait for Zesty to grow impatient enough to ask.

Zesty: "What did he do?"

Rasher: "I'm glad you asked. However, you may be sorry you did. He . . . He . . . No. It's too soon."

Hotdog: "Let me. What he did pisses in the face of thousands of years of human culture and tradition going back to the birth of agriculture and static settlements. He . . . He . . . This is harder than I thought."

Bangers: "He put the rice *in* the curry."

Everyone performs a stage gasp.

Marmalade: "But I like to mix it in myself."

Hotdog: "'It all gets mixed up together anyway.' That's what he said. The arrogant prick."

Marmalade: "But I like to mix it in myself."

Rasher: "Sssshhhhh! We know you do. Everyone does."

Hotdog: "'In some cultures, you could kill someone for that."

Bangers: "You could kill someone for it in our culture."

Marmalade: "India was furious. One billion voices shouting as one, 'Dickhead!'"

Hotdog: "Even Gandhi would have kicked him in the face."

Marmalade: "I broke up with my boyfriend shortly afterwards. It's just hard to trust again, you know?"

Rasher: "We know. I became left-handed like some kind of 17th century witch."

117

Bangers: "I got genital lice two weeks later. I'd never had it before. I've had it twice since."

Hotdog: "Just three years later, I developed an ingrown toenail. It required incredibly minor surgery. I asked the chiropodist if it could have been caused by the rice in the curry. When pressed, he said he couldn't 100% definitively prove it wasn't. So, it definitely was."

Marmalade: "It *definitely* was. Sing the song."

Zesty: "There's a song?"

Me: "Don't sing the song."

Rasher: "I don't think I should sing the s-**ONCE UPON A WHILE AGO**

Rasher bellows in a baritone that rattles the windows and everyone's chest cavities.

ONCE UPON A WHILE AGO
A LONG WAY FROM GOA
A WHITE GUY SAID TO HIMSELF
I'LL COOK A FUCKING BHUNA
HE HAD ALL THE RIGHT INGREDIENTS
THE RIGHT HERBS AND SPICES
HE HAD POPPADOMS AND TWO TYPES OF RICES
THINGS WERE LOOKING FINE
UNTIL JUST AT THE FINISH LINE
NABBING DEFEAT FROM VICTORY
HE DECIDED TO MAKE THE WHOLE MEAL SHITTY

There's an incredibly long pause here.

HE PUT THE RICE IN THE CURRY

Everyone joins in using a prissy stage whisper singing voice

He couldn't. He wouldn't.

HE PUT THE RICE IN THE CURRY
The big feckin' eegit.
HE PUT THE RICE IN THE CURRY
He's a fucking psycho
HE PUT THE RICE IN THE CURRY
What could he possibly be thinking?
HE PUT THE RICE IN THE CURRY
But I like to mix it all up myself
HE PUT THE RICE IN THE CURRY
I better ring me naan
HE PUT THE RICE IN THE CURRY LIKE A FUCKING DICKHEAD
THIS MEAL IS FUCKING BULLSHIT
The brute. The Scoundrel
HE PUT THE RICE IN THE CURRY

This goes on for four verses. When he finally finishes, there's silence as everyone looks at Zesty for her reaction. After a moment, she turns to me.

"You put the rice *in* the curry? But everyone likes to mix it up themselves." They all cheer.

"I've been to India. In some states, they'd feed you to the elephants for doing that." Zesty says

"Elephants are vegetarian." I say lamely.

"Yeah, they keep a couple specially trained to deal with special

119

dickheads." And with that, she'd won the crowd.

Later, Zesty finds me in the kitchen. The lights are off but Hotdog has lit enough candles to pray for every soul lost on the Titanic. "This is a very elaborate party." she says.

"I've been to a more elaborate one."

She smiles at me, "I can't believe you put the rice *in* the curry."

"Don't. I've been hearing about this for a decade." When people go out of their way to annihilate you with top quality abuse, you're obligated to pretend to be vexed. It's no fun for them if you don't. "They can't remember their own birthdays, but they all remember what colour socks they were wearing the day I put the rice in the curry."

"To be honest, it just sounds like you made a biryani." She confides in a stage whisper with a playful smile.

"You could have mentioned that earlier."

"What? After that song? You're on your own chef."

"Fair enough." I concede.

"I like your friends. Even Joseph in the technicolour nightmare coat."

"Yeah. We're working on that."

"That other guy is a brilliant singer. Has he written many songs?"

"Just the one."

"Seriously?"

"They were all very upset. This is the first time I've cooked for a crowd since."

"I'm glad you invited me then. The food was amazing. Thank you."

"You're very welcome."

"Prawns are actually my favourite." She says.

"Really?"

"Yeah. They were just so . . ."

"Zesty?"

"Yeah! I'm not sure about the snake and penguin though."

"Yeah. Next time I'll get some black rhinoceros"

"Aren't they extinct?"

"Oh! Em, it's frozen."

"My dad was actually in a fight to the death with a rhino while he was on safari in the Serengeti."

"What? That's amazing."

"Oh, he didn't win." she says casting her eyes downward.

"Oh! Em, sorry."

"Not really, you eejit." she laughs, giving me a playful slap on the shoulder. "You didn't strike me as being this gullible."

"Ha! Sorry. Yeah, I'm not usually. It just kinda feels like anything could happen at the moment." I say with a sincerity that would normally make me uncomfortable.

"That sounds like a nice feeling." she says matching my sincerity. There's suddenly an intimacy between us.

"It has its ups and downs." I say.

"You know my dad does actually go hunting." she whispers. "I've eaten quite a bit of rabbit and pheasant in my time." Oh balls!

"Do the rest of them know?" I ask abashed.

"The rest of them think you're Crocodile Dundee." she promises. "Your secret's safe with me."

"Thanks." This girl really is something.

She looks at me like she's making an assessment "So, what's with all the bananas?"

"I was fattening up a monkey for a Sunday roast." She laughs and it's a good laugh. She stands in closer to me. Our eyes lock. Her eyes look big in the candlelight. Brown eyes are criminally underrated in my opinion. I get a little lost in them. She leans in closer. I lean in too. Abruptly she turns away. What the actual fuck? I'm about to drop to my knees and curse this universe for its sick sense of humour when out of nowhere, she burps. The nearest candle goes out and it's suddenly slightly darker. She covers her mouth, clearly mortified.

I can't help but laugh, "I *am* a pretty good cook huh?" She punches me on the arm. Rasher's sister comes in to say goodbye. She tells me how proud she is of me. I thank her and show her out. When I come back in, Zesty asks "Why is she so proud of you?"

"Oh! Em. I've started volunteering in a charity shop." I say modestly.

"Oh, that's so nice." If there's a hell, I'll be skipping the queue and heading straight to the V.I.P section.

"Come on. We better let Rooster out of my room before Rasher vows to eat tofu for the rest of his life."

Sleeping with Strangers
A quick note on sleeping with strangers. Booze is a perfectly adequate substitute for feelings of affection or intimacy. I definitely wouldn't recommend sleeping with a stranger without it.

As soon as Rasher's sister is out the door, I neck a pineapple of rum. And eventually everyone but Zesty leaves. Hotdog wishes us a goodnight and heads off to bed. And there we are. Just the two of us. She steps up in front of me and looks up into my eyes. I'm much taller than her, which is great. I can't remember the last time someone looked at me the way she is now.

Pesto Chick

You're probably expecting more details about my encounter with Zesty but honestly, at this point, these flashbacks are out of my hands.

A sexy French witch once told me (I think she was a witch. She definitely ate frogs) that when the sex is right, it's 10% of a relationship but when it' wrong, it's 90%. With the Pesto Chick, it was never quite right. I don't think it was either of our faults. Some people just don't fit together well. I've never had problems with anyone else and I doubt she did either. She didn't give me the same benefit of the doubt. I found her intimidating. It's a sad fact that a man makes his best showing of himself when he's least determined to do so. Usually, these things go one of two ways. Things tend to happen too fast or not at all. Our issue was more complicated. And dangerous. Together we were, let's say, accident prone. Imagine The Three Stooges producing a porno and you won't be far off the mark. She nearly drowned me in the bath, and I flung her out of the shower.

Confining things to the bedroom didn't help. The floors at the Pesto Chick's place were all hardwood and she had one of those beds that inexplicably has wheels. It didn't have a headboard so if you sat up in bed, the pressure of your back against the wall would be enough to launch the bed across the room. Now imagine two fired up lovers in a lusty wrestle. It was like having sex on a skateboard. If it was possible to be sexy with a bike helmet on, we'd have gotten two. She didn't want to take the wheels off the bed in case her floors got scratched. She could be very particular about her stuff. Even after a year of living together, they were *her* floors.

Meatballs

A few days after the unbridled success which was The Turbo Exotic Barbecue, I'm on my way to the charity shop and I see Meatballs huddled in the same place again. I think about buying him another sandwich, but it's already colder than last week and the gesture is already more pathetically insufficient. To my everlasting shame, I cross the street to avoid him and proceed to curse myself until I arrive at the charity shop.

Working for charity is a bit like being a paediatric surgeon. It takes a certain kind of person to hack open a small child's chest cavity with a butcher's knife to give them a lifesaving operation. A no nonsense sociopath will get the job done while a bleeding heart, living saint falls to pieces. Pumpkin has a heart of gold. She's useless. A lot of people strong-arm her into discounts and lumber her with some truly hideous rubbish rather than find an unguarded bonfire to dump it in. She just can't say no. I'm a natural. It's the majority of the work I plan on doing in the shop. I do not fold anything.

I find her in the process of dressing five new mannequins. It's a fucking horror show. They're too realistic.

The Uncanny Valley
If something looks a little bit lifelike, you attribute a human connection to it and it's cute, like a teddy bear, but if it gets too realistic, you stop seeing it as an inanimate object doing a good job of appearing lifelike, you start to hold it to the same standard as a person. You stop seeing where it succeeds and only where it fails. It creeps you the fuck out.

These dummies are just too real while not being nearly real enough, like Hollywood sex symbols from the 80s after the plastic surgery.

"You're never going to sell anything those goblins are wearing." I point out completely skipping the hello.

"Are they that bad?" she frets while taking a step back to access her handy work.

"Those two look like Sloth from The Goonies had a queer eye makeover and Cher the day after one of her bi-annual facelifts. They're gonna scare people out of the shop. And why are their nipples so massive?"

"They were donated. Someone left them outside last night." she says, adjusting Cher's blouse in a vain effort to hide her dagger nips.

"How do you know they didn't walk here by themselves in search of souls to feed on? Those two look like Harrison Ford had his face cut off and had to have a skin graft from his huge, saggy ball-sack stretched over his entire head and that one's like Arnold Schwarzenegger in Total Recall when his head starts to explode."

"Oh dear. Do you think we should get rid of them then?" she says while wringing her lands, looking genuinely tormented, bless her.

"This one looks like Sonia from EastEnders after she wore a beehive as a motorbike helmet. She'll haunt children's dreams. She also has inexplicably giant nipples."

"OK, OK. I'll get rid of them."

"I can sort it for you?" I suggest.

"Really? You don't mind? That'd be great. Thank you."

After being incredibly rude to a man with a bowl cut (Curried Egg) who definitely didn't need another cardigan, I go to find Meatballs sitting in his usual spot.

"Hello." I say.

"Hi." he replies timidly.

"How are you doing?"

"Not great, but things could always be worse." he says with a smile. I'm not this upbeat on my best day and I live inside.

"Yeah?" I ask dubiously.

"Yeah. It's important to stay positive, you know? If you put good energy out into the world, good things will come back to you. Karma, you know?"

Christ!

"OK. Look, I'd like to help you." I say.

"You're very kind and I do appreciate a sandwich, but what I really need is a job."

"Come on." I tell him.

He looks dubious for a second before shrugging and following me. I lead him around the back of the charity shop where I've stashed them. The five creepiest fashion mannequins in the world are dressed in old jeans, old hoodies and old shoes. With the hoods up, they look less like they're moments away from coming to life and peeling your skin off to better pass off as one of us.

"I don't get it. You want me to work at the charity shop?"

"No. What you do is set these dummies up sitting on the ground around town with collection plates. Then, all you have to do is go around collecting the money people give them. You'll have to rearrange them a bit when no one's looking so it looks like they're moving. You can get five times as much as you are now."

He moves towards the plastic horrors and gives them a closer inspection. "No one will believe these are real people. They look like the Nazis when their faces melted off when they opened the Arc of The Covenant."

126

"When was the last time anyone looked at you?" I ask more harshly than I meant to.

"Good point." he agrees with a sad nod.

"With their hoods up and heads down, no one will notice a thing."

"Isn't this a bit, I don't know, questionable? Morally?"

"That depends. Are you cold?"

"Yeah."

"Are you hungry?"

"Yeah."

"Are you sleeping outside tonight?"

"Yes."

"Then, it's fine. People are still choosing to help you. Now, more people will have the opportunity. Same principal. You're just expanding. You're basically Robin Hood. You're taking from the rich and giving to the poor. Listen, in this world, you can either rip the piss or have the piss ripped out of you. Fair is for fairy tales. If Karma was real, most of us would be dead. You can sit about waiting for justice if you like, but wouldn't you rather wait in a nice flat? This society is a fucking joke. If you lose your job and have no one to mooch off, you're homeless. That's it. There's no safety net."

"That's what happened to me. I got made redundant, found another job, but it fell through at the last minute and then I was suddenly just outside."

"You played by the rules and society fucked you. People don't care about people. People care about dogs. You can't wait for help. It won't come. You need to help yourself. Get creative."

What could he say? We carry each dummy to a different corner like we're supporting a drunk friend and set them up. Meatballs thanks me and I wish him luck. I'm feeling pretty good about the whole thing. Saving humanity is a project worthy of my dedication.

127

The Clinic

The next morning, I wake up to Rooster's dawn serenade. Running into the living room, I throw *The Sun Also Rises* at him. I stumble into my flip-flops and stagger towards the bathroom. Hotdog growls as he comes out. I snarls at him. He doesn't do the morning time either. I have the taste of hotdogs in my mouth. I shrug and head for the bathroom. I urinate . . . battery acid.

What the actual fuck? A sound like a distinctly effeminate, wounded animal escapes my throat. What coul-. Zesty! You fruity harlot! Apparently, an apple a day kept the sexual health doctor away. By the time I finish this fire piss, I'm on the verge of tears.

I get dressed and head to the clap clinic. I'm able to taste the sandwich of everyone I encountered on the way. You really never appreciate your health until you're unwell. My whole sandwich thing has been consistent since it first started, except when I'm sick. Things get strange when I'm sick. I had scarlet fever once and for two weeks I could tell what peoples' allergies were. Legitimate gluten intolerance is incredibly rare. Another time, I had a bad case of the flu, and I suddenly knew what everyone's favourite type of crisps were. I've never met a Ready Salted person I liked.

The clinic isn't even open when I arrive. Time does not fly when you've got a radioactive crotch. After a thousand years or so, a tired looking nurse (Egg Mayonnaise) Christ! I can taste it! comes along and opens up. I'm sitting in the waiting area for ages, ashamed of my life. I pick up an old newspaper to hide behind and look at the crossword page. I probably could have made a good go of it if the Eggy Mayo hadn't confiscated my pen the instant I filled out my forms. Then, I have a quick look at the cryptic clues.

128

Anyone who has ever gotten even one of these should immediately be committed to an asylum for the criminally deranged. Eventually the nurse calls me in. As she looks down at the form I've filled out, she asks. "So, Mr . . . Kenobi? Sorry, you do know that this is strictly confidential right?" She's already fed up.

"Yes." I say sheepishly.

She rolls her eyes, "Right, well, what brings you here bright and early this morning?"

"What? Well, she's Caucasian, brunette, 5.3, about 28."

"I mean," she interrupts "Are you here for a check-up or are you experiencing symptoms?"

"Oh! Yes. Symptoms. Sorry." My face is burning nearly as much as my dick.

"And?" she rolls her finger, gesturing for me to continue.

"I don't know the technical nomenclature for this type of thing."

"Layman's terms will suffice Obi Wan." There's an impatient edge to her voice. Nonsense isn't for everyone.

"Well, I'm pissing lightning bolts."

"A burning sensation whilst urinating?"

"Yes. That. Sorry."

"Have you recently had unprotected sex with a new partner?"

"Err, yes. Sort of. I didn't mean to. I held this barbecue and there were fruity drinks in pineapples, and she burped out a candle and one thing just kinda led to another." A grown man shouldn't be bashful.

"I see. The aforementioned Caucasian brunette? We'll take a blood and urine sample but from your eloquent description, I think it's safe to say you have Chlamydia, so we can start you on an antibiotic straight away."

"What will become of me?" I might sound a tad dramatic, but this is a terrible affliction.

"You should be cured in seven days."

Oh! "Yeah? Wow! That's amazing. Science is so underrated."

"Is it? Most people agree science is pretty good." She's oozing sarcasm, but I'm too relieved to care.

"Is there anything I can do for the pain while peeing in the meantime?"

"The best thing you can do is pee in the bath."

"What? How is that different from peeing in a toilet?"

A slow deep sigh escapes her lips before she says, "No. What you do is run a hot bath, get in and then pee."

"Like R. Kelly? You're not serious?"

"As serious as The Sith Obi-Wan."

I taste everyone's sandwich on the way home. I go back and forth between delight and disgust until my brain starts to crackle.

Later, Hotdog and I are back at the bonfire site watching the flames as my sheets burn.

"So, did they give you anything for your sexy disease?" He asks with the bare minimum of sympathy.

"Yeah, I got antibiotics and I'm supposed to piss myself in the bath."

"What?" he laughs, "Like R. Kelly?"

"Yeah."

"Can you clean the bath afterwards please?"

When the only response this provokes is a sigh, he tries, "Are you going to see her again?"

"I don't know. She's literally growing on me."

Flat Rat

The following evening, I'm sitting in my room working out the logistics of forging old messages in antique bottles with antique coins for Beetroot to find on the beach with his metal detector and thinking about setting up mint bushes and individual greenhouses for lime trees for renewable Mojito stations when I hear an unmanly roar from the living room. I run out to find Hotdog standing on the kitchen table much like how I had done on my bed.

"What are you doing up there?"

"There's a rat in the flat!" he bellows.

As we stand shoulder to shoulder on the kitchen table, we weigh our options.

"Where is it?" I ask.

"Behind the sofa."

"Was it huge?"

"I think it was a baby one." he says with a quiver in his voice.

"What? How do you know it wasn't a really big mouse?"

"I'm not Dave Attenborough. Rat in the flat or mouse in the house. Does it matter?"

"No, you're right. I apologise. What are we gonna do?"

"We can't afford to stay in a hotel."

"I am owed a couple of favours. I can probably borrow a cat?"

"Good thinking . . . Well? Go on then." He gives me the 'why aren't you already out of the bloody door' glare.

"What? Now? How would you suggest I go about that?"

He thinks for a second before suggesting, "The floor is lava?"

"Of course! You stay here and keep an eye on the sofa to make sure it doesn't move."

Using two chairs as stilts, I make my way over to the sink and climb out the kitchen window. I return later with Cat and climb back in the window to find Hotdog still standing on the kitchen table but playing a flute.

"What are you doing? Are you fucking Pied Pipering?"

The Pied Piper of Hamelin
The Pied Piper of Hamelin is a folktale about a pest control officer who first deals with a rat infestation problem before kidnapping 130 children. If this story has a moral, I've never figured it out.

"What? No. I'm just playing so it knows I'm still here so it won't come out. I was talking to it, but it got a bit weird. I was starting to confide in it." Hotdog looks at his shoes. I'd be embarrassed too.

"Yeah, you've sidestepped weird alright." I tell him.

"Why did you climb in and out of the window?" he counters.

"Shut up!"

I set Cat loose to hunt. Two minutes later, there are two grown men and a cat on the kitchen table.

"Great cat." says Hotdog clearly unimpressed.

"He used to be a lot braver."

"Any more brilliant ideas?"

"No. We need a snake to flush it out and an owl to finish the job."

"Wait! Do you think Rooster could take it?"

"Have you got your Interweb phone on you?"

"Interweb phone?"

"Jesus! Save the techno babble for later. Do you have it? I demand.

"Yeah. Why?"

"Ask Jeeves."

"Ask him what?"

"If a rooster with a history of violence can take a rat in a battle to the death." I say through gritted teeth.

"History of violence? What are you talking about?"

"Rooster's from the wrong side of the farmyard alright. Just do it."

The table creeks. We look at each other in horror. Hotdog holds Cat while I parkour my way over to the bathroom and open the door. Rooster bursts out like a fucking velociraptor and heads straight for the sofa.

There Are No Words

There are no words is a rubbish exclamation used by kids these days. There are words. Kids are just inarticulate and lazy.

I'm sure there are words to describe the horror we witnessed. I'm too traumatised to weave them together. It was nothing like *Pokémon*. The bloodbath that followed will haunt us both until we die. We stay on the kitchen table long after the flat rat/house mouse has been dispatched, standing side by side, staring at Rooster as he struts back and forth in front of us. Eventually, without turning to me, Hotdog whispers "He's a cold-blooded killer!"

Enunciating every syllable slowly and clearly, I whisper back, "Do *not* take your hands off that fucking cat."

It takes half a dozen flung books on growing prize-winning vegetables to herd Rooster back into the bathroom. On our way to return Cat to Brie, we stop off at the bonfire site to cremate the body of the interloper. As we watch the pyre burn down, Hotdog says, "Mate?"

"Yes mate?"

"This fire business is getting out of hand."

"Yeah, there are druids out there doing this less than us. This should probably be the last one, yeah?"

"After we get rid of the rotten picnic bench from the yard though?"

"Yeah, after we get rid of the rotten picnic bench from the yard." I agree.

"Mate?"

"Yes mate?"

"I feel we handled that with great aplomb."

For a moment, I'm too exasperated to say anything before eventually managing "Let's get this cat home."

Brie

The thing you need to know about Brie's place is that it's arty as fuck. There's animal skulls and black and white photography all over the place. When her brother graduated from university, her parents bought him a car. When Brie graduated, they offered to buy her one too. She declined but asked for an antique Armenian rug instead. It doesn't fly or anything. Having a work of art decorating the floor in a room where gallons of red wine are guzzled on a weekly basis makes for some high-octane boozing. We drink Malbec on a knifes edge. The stakes are high. Even treading on this carpet is like licking The Mona Lisa's forehead. Spilling red wine on it is like punching a small Armenian child in the face. Whenever there's a spill, it's all hands on deck. Everyone runs around like headless chickens throwing baking soda, vinegar, washing powder, battery acid and holy water on the stain, working in into a lather of regret. Then we all wax on, wax off until we get bored or thirsty. It's all very stressful, though not stressful enough to get us to make the switch to Chardonnay.

Brie greets us at her door with her customary glass of wine in hand.

"Our fearless hunters and their faithful, furry friend return. Have you brought a feast or are you two coming to live with me forever?"

"Our hunt was successful." Hotdog declares. "We have vanquished the beast."

"It was massive actually." I say, "By one account we comported ourselves with great aplomb. Please thank your friend for letting us borrow her cat. It was worse than useless."

"Yeah, I'll get him home tomorrow. Aplomb huh? Wow! You

135

both look like you have shellshock. Come in and help me drink this wine. It amazes me; cavemen hunted woolly mammoths, cave lions and sabretooth tigers and bears. Fast forward fifteen thousand years and you two blousy shirts are afraid of a hamster.

"Rats spread the black plague which killed 60% of Europe's population between 1347 and 1351" blurts Hotdog intensely, but historically accurately.

"And mice?" she prods.

"Yes."

"And hamsters? Gerbils? Guinea Pigs? Chinchillas?" she pesters.

"Yes, yes, fuckedy yes, yes. All of them except squirrels." Hotdog insists.

"Yeah, except squirrels." I agree.

"And you're afraid of swans." she aims at me.

"One broke my arm." I protest. "Did you know that they live between twenty and thirty years? Thirty-three in captivity. Why would they need to live that long? The suspicious fuckers. They're protected by law despite not being endangered. It used to be treason to kill one. Tell me that doesn't sound like political manoeuvring."

"You may have mentioned it once or twice, yes." She turns to Hotdog. "Aren't you scared of long-life milk?"

"It's fucking radioactive! Neither man nor milk were meant to live forever. We're soaring too close to the sun." he declares a tad dramatically though I agree wholeheartedly.

"We could hunt a sabretooth tiger. If we had proper spears." I say, thinking out loud.

"We'd need a good source of flint." says Hotdog.

"You can get it wherever there's gravel apparently. We could get some from the old quarry by the roundabout."

"We'd need oak or ash for the shafts."

"There's a few oaks growing by the river. We could harden the tips in fire before attaching the flint heads."

Brie butts in, "Have you guys ever seen any of those documentaries about couples who murder together?"

"We only watch films from the 80s and 90s." I say.

"I've always wondered how these people find each other."

"What's your point?" Hotdog asks.

"Never mind." Bored of our nonsense, Brie changes the subject again.

"Glass of wine?"

"Sure." Hotdog says agreeably. She goes out to the kitchen and comes back with a bottle in one hand and three glasses in the other.

I perform The Cough of Implication.

She rolls her eyes and walks back into the kitchen muttering something about being "sick of this Peter Pan bullshit."

We sit around the dining table drinking wine from a gravy boat, a tea pot and a plastic skull bowl for holding sweets at Halloween. She'd lost to me at Buckaroo a while back and her forfeit was to owe me "Three Reasonable Favours". My first was to always be served drinks in something more interesting than a glass or cup. I used the second one tonight borrowing Cat. I'm saving my last one for something special.

"So, what's new with you two?" she asks.

"He's got chlamydia." Hotdog announces unnecessarily while pointing at me.

"Judas!" Annoyed, I fold my arms over my chest, sit back and with the arch of an eyebrow and out of spite say, "He's gay."

"Oh! I . . . can't believe it?" Brie stutters to Hotdog without an ounce of conviction.

"I hope you'll still look at me the same way." Hotdog is sickeningly sincere.

"I'm sure I'll manage darling. What's brought all this on?"

Sparing no detail, Hotdog proceeds to regale Brie with a supernatural tale of a haunted board game not for the faint of heart. When he finishes, she says, "That's amazing. We need to celebrate. Fancy going to the corner shop and grabbing another bottle?"

"Yeah. Great!" He agrees.

When Hotdog pops out, she looks at me for a long moment. When she eventually speaks, there's more curiosity than accusation in her voice. "How ... How did you do the 'hell's bells'?"

"I set the alarm on my phone to vibrate and put it in one of those old hand bells. I think it was from a school or something originally."

"Ahhh!" She's quiet again for a bit. "So, you gave him permission to be gay then?"

"I wouldn't put it like that."

She folds her arms which is never a happy sign. "He proper thinks he's witnessed a miracle."

"He believed in it all anyway, but now he doesn't think he's going to hell."

"I don't know about this. Whatever in the world gave you the notion?"

"Well, I went metal detecting wit-"

"Of course!" she interrupts, "I keep telling you. That idiot isn't a sage, guru, hermit doling out wisdom to lost souls. He's a lunatic."

"He encouraged me to open myself up to the possibilities, put myself out in the world and see what happens."

138

She goes silent again for a moment before asking, "Did you know that before they tested the first nuclear bomb, they had no idea what would happen? They weren't sure it wouldn't ignite the entire atmosphere."

"I'm not likely to burn the world down. Sitting about thinking all the time hasn't gotten me anywhere."

"How far has action gotten you?" she asks, unconvinced.

"I'm out of the house. Out of myself."

She chews on her top lip before blurting, "Fuck it. Let's see what happens." she brightens, "That's a really nice thing you've done for him. You know, I haven't seen him this happy since we hit puberty. He actually looks more handsome."

"Isn't it weird?"

"You're a good friend."

"I made him think God wants him to do all the washing up." I admit.

"Nobody said you were a saint. What's he going to do with his big cash settlement?"

"Oh, he's already traded that cash cow for some magic, pervert beans."

"And you seem better? Look at the two of you out in the world having what could loosely be considered a borderline adventure."

"Well, I have stopped crying in the shower."

"Oh? Have you started taking long, sad baths?"

"You're funny." I say, deadpan.

"Yes. I am." Her deadpan is far superior to mine.

"Things are looking up." I say, topping up our glasses. The glug of the booze makes me want to pee, but I'll need more Dutch courage before I can face it. "I think I just needed a project."

"You are a man of many projects. What have you landed on?"

"I'm gonna make the world a better place." I announce with as little gravitas as possible.

She laughs, "Is that all? Are you gonna build an orphanage in the third world or save the giraffes?"

"I just wanna make some noise. I wanna make things a lot more interesting around here."

"That sounds like something a super-villain would say at the start of the film."

"It does a bit, doesn't it? Wait! Why would the giraffes need saving? Who's bothering the giraffes?"

"I heard something on the radio about giraffe meat being sold locally. There's some kind of investigation looking into it."

Oh fuck! I try harder at the deadpan. "Oh? That's strange."

"Yeah, apparently there's been a huge influx of donations to some giraffe conservation charity. What kind of person would eat a giraffe?"

"You'd be amazed by how many people wouldn't even raise an eyebrow at the idea of eating a giraffe."

"Well, anyway, I believe in you."

"You do?" I ask, surprised.

"Yeah, that's why I've been so bitterly disappointed in you all these years." This is either a rubbish compliment or a brilliant insult.

"Thanks?"

"You're welcome."

Hotdog comes back in with a bottle of red in each hand. Brie changes the subject. "Anyway. Chlamydia, huh?"

"Just a bit. Please don't tell anyone."

"Oh darling." she says in her most sickly sweet and patronising tone. "I'm obviously going to have to tell *every*one. You know that."

140

"Yeah. I know." My shoulders drop but what choice does she have?

"Was it someone special?"

"She's popular anyway. Apparently."

"He has to piss himself in the bath." says Hotdog.

"Like R. Kelly?" Brie laughs.

"Yeah." I admit.

"You like her?" she asks.

"She's infected me. Like, not in an emotional way."

"But do you like her?" she pesters.

"She's managed to contrive this notion in her head that deep down I'm a good person." I tell her.

"I think the drill bit would melt long before you got that deep darling. What did she say when you confronted her?"

"When I what?"

"Come on. You have to tell her."

"Wait. What? It's my responsibility to tell her that she gave me a sexy disease? What kinda social convention is that? What if she doesn't believe me and accuses me of giving it to her?" My palms are sweaty just at the thought of such a conversation.

"Look," she says, "if you want to be part of civilisation, you have to conform to certain cultural obligations."

"Are telegrams still a thing?" I ask.

"How terrible is it?"

"Chlamydia? It's like pissing boiling orange juice. With the bits in. After it's been through a SodaStream."

"Graphic!" she grimaces.

Sick of my penis problems, I ask her, "What's happening with you? Are you still seeing whatshisface?"

"Christ! Just about. Tell me, at what point *exactly* does spending time with someone go from being this whimsical, magical

141

gift that you mutually give each other to being something they're bloody entitled to, I'm obliged to give, and they can whinge incessantly about it if I'm not in the mood to give it? And how do I avoid ever making this transition ever again?"

"That's an excellent question." I concede.

"And?" Her eyes are as big as saucers as she demands an answer.

"And you're asking us two? We know more about hunting woolly mammoths."

"Who is this?" asks Hotdog completely lost.

"He's a Yo-Yo champion. With a moustache." I tell him.

"Have you seen *her*?" Brie counters in what I feel is a completely disproportionate response.

"Who?" I ask, not sounding as baffled as I'd intended.

"You know exactly who fucker. The Whore of Babylon."

"The River Wench of Hades?" adds Hotdog.

"The Dreaded Bridge Troll of The Shadows."

"The Poison Serpent of Septic Tanks."

"The Banshee of Sodom."

"The Abolisher of Smiles."

"Oh! *Her*!" I cut in. These two could go back and forth all night. "Yeah, I saw her. Briefly." I say as casual as possible, inspecting my fingernails, convincing no one.

"And?" Brie presses.

"It's a long story."

"How long?"

"About fifteen pages."

"You're not the first idiot to waste his energies trying to make a miserable bitch happy. You should have set your sights on something slightly less ambitious. Like being a rock star."

"On Mars." Chimes in Hotdog unhelpfully.

"Or a professional football player." she goes again.

"Who wins an Oscar."

"And a Nobel prize."

"Or a lion tamer."

"On a helicopter." Brie finishes and they high five which is something I've never seen either of them do before. I'd forgotten that Hotdog could be a bit witty when he wasn't moping. Two against one really is horrific odds.

"Fuck off guys. What's wrong with trying to make someone happy? Surely that's a selfless, noble thing to do?"

"Hunting for self-validation by trying to prove yourself to a horrible bastard isn't as beneficent as you might think." says Hotdog.

"You're suddenly very insightful for a guy whose sexual awakening is as fresh and sure-footed as a wobbly, new-born foal."

Friends

Have as many mates, pals and buddies as you like, but don't overdo it with friends. They'll know you. They'll know the fuck out of you. And they'll be honest with you even when you specifically request they not be.

Borderline emotionally nauseous from this, I change the subject and say to Brie "How's the new, big career going?" Brie has explained what she does for a living too many times for us to ask her again, so we only ever speak of her job in the vaguest terms.

"It's good, though I was in theatre today for hours and then I had a conference with the engineers." What the hell does she do?

"And obviously this weather we're having complicates things."

"Obviously." No idea.

143

"It's the commute that's a killer though. I get in the car at six in the morning and I'm often not home until after eight in the evening."

"I don't know how you do it." says Hotdog. "I'd struggle to stay awake behind the wheel."

"Well, actually," she says with a little laugh, "I have found a practical life hack to overcome that issue."

"You're not drinking those energy drinks, are you?" I ask, worried "They're radioactive camel piss."

"No."

"Norwegian death metal?" Hotdog guesses.

"No."

"Smoking crack?"

"Stop fucking guessing! I've actually been" she coughs, "you know." She looks down at her crotch.

It takes me a moment to get it, "You're joking!"

"If I was joking, you'd be laughing darling."

"What?" asks Hotdog.

"I've bee-"

"She's been wanking in the car on the way to work!" I declare like I'm exposing the killer in a murder mystery.

"That's disgusting." says Hotdog scrunching his nose.

"I have antibacterial wipes in the glovebox." she protests haughtily.

"Still."

"13% of drivers admit to falling asleep at the wheel in this country every year. It's wank or be killed out there!" she says seriously. She has more in common with us than she'd like to admit.

"Don't people overtaking ... see you?" I ask.

"No. They only see you from the chest up."

"Wait! What about truck drivers? They must be able to see

144

down into the car?" Hotdog points out.

"Oh, truck drivers can absolutely see me, but then I zoom past, and they're gone forever. Seeing me probably wakes them up too."

"I'm sure it does. Incredible" To the untrained eye, Brie comes across as the rational, reasonable one, but she's as mad as any of them. "Anyway, we're going trolling for dudes Friday night if you wanna come? I'm going for immoral support."

"Oh great! Wait! Who else is going?" She asks suspiciously.

Her fears are well founded. She's no fan of Bangers, but he is the closest thing we have to a lady's man, which is the closest thing we have to a man's man.

"Errrmmm" I hesitate a moment too long.

Her nostrils actually flare as she realises who I'm omitting. "I'm not going anywhere with that degenerate." she snaps.

"He's not that bad." I say. Actually, he is.

"I've known that creep for fifteen years and he still comes onto me every time I see him. Getting into that fucker's friend zone is harder than infiltrating North Korea. Plus, he's got unclaimed bastards all over town."

"What? You can't just make unfounded claims like that." I say, defending my savage friend.

"Unfounded? There's miniature clones of him all over the place. With beady eyes and the curls of the devil."

"He's definitely made a splash in the local gene pool." Hotdog agrees.

"The gene pool in this town is more of a stagnant puddle. We all look the same." I don't know why I'm disagreeing. I'm utterly convinced.

"He doesn't." she insists, "Also, the last time I saw him he was sitting on a public bench outside a pub on his laptop mooching Wi-Fi."

"So?"

"He was watching porn. He complained about the signal. The time before that, I asked if he'd help me carry drinks back from the bar. His exact response was 'I would do anything for you . . . or *to* you.'"

I turn to Hotdog, "Just the three of us then I think."

After we finish the wine, Brie coaxes us to the pub around the corner to catch last orders. It's a proper old man's boozer. I wasn't about in the 70s but if I had been, I feel I would have known that laying carpet in a pub was never going to be a good idea. The one in here has recorded every bad decision that's been made since. We're sitting there sipping our drinks, trying to piece together what Brie does for a living without coming right out and asking when she suddenly downs her gin and turns to me "Are you ready?"

"For wha-? Realisation slaps me right in the balls. "Oh no! Please don't."

She smiles at me and says bye to Hotdog. The smile turns to fury as she stands up and shouts in my face, "You *are* going to die in my arms. Now, whether that happens peacefully in your sleep, surrounded by our great grandkids fifty years from now or down an alley behind the bins later this week is entirely up to you."

With that, she turns on her heels and storms out leaving me and Hotdog to be gawked at by the whole bar. Turns out she's a shark at Connect 4 but getting to do this every time we see each other really doesn't seem like a Reasonable Request in hind-spite.

The next morning, when Rooster begins massacring the dawn chorus, I don't get up to chuck a book at him. Neither does Hotdog. After last night's display of violence, it seems he's in charge now.

Out Out

Heaven help us, but that Friday night is Hotdog's introduction to the gay community. Terrified of what he'll throw together, I end up choosing his outfit, despite knowing nothing about fashion. Up until five years ago, I was still rocking an eyebrow piercing like it was 1992, but what I pick for him doesn't require putting sunblock on my eyeballs to look at him, plus we're both clean, so I'd say that qualifies us as looking sharp.

Bangers turns up at our place a full hour earlier than arranged with an entire case of expired blue flavoured alcopops and declares, "If you're not drinking with both hands tonight, you better be wanking." The savage won't say where he got them from, but in no time, our brains are crackling from the sugar high, and our stomachs feel like they're full of battery acid. We're so hyped up on sugar, artificial colours and white spirits that we're suddenly really excited to be going out out.

We walk to the club. There's an energy in the air that reminds me of my first school disco. I think it's the nervousness radiating off of Hotdog. It seems to have infected me and Bangers too. I think he might even still be wearing Lynx Africa. He's especially giddy. If he had a tail, it would definitely be wagging. "Lock up your daughters. We're fucking serial killers!" he bellows at the moon before side glancing at Hotdog and amending, "Oh! And lock up your sons too. We'll murder them as well."

"That's very inclusive of you." I say. Hotdog is subdued and starts to lag behind, "What do I say? What do I do?" he frets.

"Relax." Bangers reassures him, "It's just a bunch of dudes you're gonna be coming onto. We're not exactly famous for playing

147

hard to get now, are we?" I'm not sure if this qualifies as offensive or not?

"I suppose." he still sounds doubtful.

"Yeah, just be yourself." I suggest, slapping him on the shoulders. "You're handsome and brave. These guys are gonna love you."

We arrive and have to queue outside for the best part of twenty minutes. Overhearing snippets of mindless conversations taking place around us in the queue makes me suspicious that I may be too sober for this. I'm definitely too old for it.

After we pay to get in, which is something I haven't done in ten years, we head inside looking for the bar. It's so dark, they're definitely trying to hide the place more so than set a mood. It smells like ten thousand Friday nights and the floor is so sticky, my shoes nearly come off. I absolutely need more booze for this. I notice all the kids in here. All the boys are wearing the exact same shirt and have the exact same haircut, while all the girls are pretty much naked in tiny dresses. I'm definitely too old for discotheques. Without even asking the lads what they want, I wade through the crowd to the bar to get the drinks in.

When I turn around, drinks in hand, I spot the two love machines at a table overlooking the dance floor. It's one of those dance floors with the lights flashing in it like in *Saturday Night Fever*.

Saturday Night Fever

Saturday Night Fever is a 1977 film starring John Travolta. The soundtrack features four songs by The Bee Gees and probably the most iconic dancing scenes in film. It's Brilliant!

Absolutely no one will be breakdancing on that Petri dish though. Hotdog and Bangers are deep in conversation when I reach the

148

table and Bangers is mid rant, shouting over the booming pop anthem rattling the whole place. "It's easy for boring, nice people to be nice all the time. Where's the fucking merit in that? Try being a prick and constantly trying to fight it. As soon as I let my guard down even for a second, I'm a monster. It's like having to keep a muscle constantly flexed."

"That's pretty profound for you buddy." Hotdog shouts back at him. I thought so too if I'm honest.

"Or maintain a rock-hard erection at all times."

"There it is." Hotdog laughs. Jesus!

I put down the drinks and head straight to the toilet in hopes of bypassing this conversation entirely. It's early but I still have to navigate the men's room on tippy toes and try to stay in the shallow end. My piss isn't blue, which is a relief. By the time I get back, they've both completely abandoned ship, leaving their drinks on the table. I spot Hotdog with his tongue down the throat of a tiny man (Pulled Pork) in the corner.

Bangers is on the dance floor harassing strangers. He's started on the left-hand side and is systematically making his way across the floor, approaching every girl in his path. The animal doesn't even seem to have a preference. I can't read lips, but I know his one chat up line, and I can clearly see that he's going up to each one and shouting over the booming Pink song that's playing "I've got a nine-inch tongue and I can breathe through my ears." before sticking his tongue out to prove it. Say what you like about Bangers, but that monster does have a tongue like a fucking Komodo dragon. He could lick Bolognese off his own eyebrows. I briefly consider telling him that it's blue from all the alcopops but decide against it. Watching him on the pull is a bit like watching a nature documentary. I can nearly hear David Attenborough providing commentary.

149

"Bangers approaches and begins to circle the herd seeking out its weakest member, but the herd knows that to make eye contact would spell their doom, and that strength lies in their numbers. The gazelles tighten their circle as they dance around their handbags with their backs to their predator. He circles, searching, hoping to isolate the young or the old. Either would be fine. He doesn't give a fuck. Eventually he spots weakness, and he strikes. That poor girl will be lucky to get out of this with her life and just a two minute incredibly awkward conversation."

Of course, the trouble with nature documentaries is that it's all about perspective. In last week's episode, we followed the gazelle and hoped she could outrun the lion. This week, we're following that same lion and hoping he eats that same gazelle. I don't know who I'm backing tonight. I'd like to see my friend meet someone. He might be a sleazy savage but this whole scene is what he settles for. I don't think it's what he's looking for. At the same time, these poor, innocent young ladies have their whole lives ahead of them.

I decide I'll have these three drinks before going home by myself like in a Smiths' song. Hotdog is a bloody natural. He doesn't need a wing man. Just then, an honest to God sexy goth chick (Fish Fingers) steps up to me. I haven't seen a proper sexy goth in years. She stands there staring at me looking characteristically unhappy about something.

"Hi?" I say like an idiot.

"Not yet."

"What?"

"You're not gay." she accuses.

"Oh! Em," panicking for something to say, I come out with, "I'm Sapio/Demi/Pan/Poly/Uni sexual. Tonight, I'm ironically portraying a hetero normative alpha male as an artistic commentary on the societal construct of toxic masculinity." What am I talking about?

"Oh! I see. That explains your outfit."

"It does?"

"You'll need a partner then." She sits down.

"Em, yeah. So, what are you doing here?"

"Waiting."

"Waiting?" I'm lost.

"For you."

"For me?"

"You're late!"

"I'm late?"

She slaps me across the face.

"JESUS! What's your name?" I ask.

"Let's not put labels on this." At this point, neither her face nor her body language have even hinted at an emotion.

"I'm feeling intimidated." I admit.

She puts her index finger over my lips. "Don't *tell* me. *Show* me."

"Err" Maintaining eye contact with this woman is starting to make my retinas sting.

"Do you bruise easily?" she asks.

"Only emotionally." She still has her fingers over my lips.

"That will suffice."

"ANK OOOHHH." I gargle with three goth girl fingers now in my mouth. Her fingers taste like cheese and onion crisps. Not very sexy. Or goth. I would have just assumed that salt and vinegar would be the go-to crisp of the pasty children of the night. What kind of biscuits would a goth eat? My gut instinct wants to say ginger nut. She's saying something. Was that a question? She's still talking. Fuck! What the hell is she talking about? She looks expectant. Say something. "No?" I guess.

"Good. Doing this kinda thing is very dangerous if you have asthma. Or epilepsy. Or diabetes."

Fuck!

"Do you mind if we watch porn while we mate?" she continues.

"Are you bored of me already?"

"What?" she snaps. A burst of rage counts as an emotion, right?

"I'm joking. That's not mental at all."

Am I really gonna get drunk enough to tolerate this harpy's company? And body fluids? Believe it or not, I'm not really into hardcore, sadomasochistic sex play and even though The Pesto Chick worked in a sex toy shop, she wasn't either. There was an incident however.

Super-Soaker

We kept a strict closed bathroom door policy. I have no interest in that level of intimacy, but at her sister's wedding last year, something happened. You should have seen her in her bridesmaid's dress though. She was like a lilac angel. We had a room in the hotel where the reception was held, and we'd gone upstairs so she could change out of her heels. Her feet didn't hurt. She just didn't want to dance with me if she was taller than me. The Pesto Chick always worried about other peoples' opinions. It was an open-bar and we'd taken advantage. By the time we got to the room, we were both desperate to pee. She bolted for the toilet, and I was hot on her heels. She was peeing while I danced a jig in front of her and harassed her to hurry up. This would never cross the minds of sober people, but she said fuck it and told me to pee between her legs. In my blind panic, I thought this was a brilliant idea.

Her dress was ruined. So was her make-up. I don't know why R. Kelly is so into it. It was horrible. I never heard the end of it. The Pesto Chick has a great memory. I guess you could say I've been a bit obsessive about my aim ever since.

The Craft

I snap out of it and this child of the night is somehow still talking. "I've had it adapted so it runs off the mains now instead of batteries which is actually illegal everywhere except Slovenia."

Christ! What the fuck is this deviant talking about? Focus!

"That's the safe word. I won't break character or turn my equipment off for anything else, no matter how much you beg or scream. Do we have an accord?"

An accord? I didn't catch a word of that.

"Yeah. Great." I say.

"Good. I'm going to take a slash. I'll be back. Don't you fucking move."

She abruptly sticks her tongue down my throat and saunters off. Yep. Cheese and onion. I watch her walk away. If this harpy touches my penis, I'm gonna let her keep it. Bangers plops down in the seat beside me, takes his drink and downs it.

"My mouth is so dry." he complains.

"You've had your tongue out since we got here." I point out.

"You've gotta let the ladies know what you're offering. Where is he?"

I point, "He's kissing that tiny man in the corner."

"Oh! Wow! Look at him go! Handsy and all. Fair play to him. Look at that little fella's beard. It's so trimmed, it looks like it's drawn on with a marker. I didn't think that'd be his type at all."

"What did you think his type would be?" I ask.

"I don't know. Someone more like me, I suppose."

"What made you think that?"

"What? Did you think he'd go for someone more like you?"

"I really don't know what you wanna hear right now. How's it going out there?"

"Not great. So far." That 'so far' is the difference between me and Bangers. He's a believer.

"I better get back out there. You never know your luck in a small town."

"I don't know how you do it." I tell him with a strange blend of admiration and horror.

"You know what my philosophy is?"

"If you can't lift her, don't shift her?"

"No."

"If you can't hide her, don't ride her?"

"No."

"Don't screw the crew, unless you can?"

"Stop fucking guessing! My philosophy is that getting rejected by a stranger who doesn't know me and is in no way qualified to judge me is never going to hurt my feelings. And in the same way, I don't know her either. Maybe she's into some fucked up shit that I can't cater for. Maybe she only likes cross-eyed, horsey guys, you know, that could eat apples through a letterbox. I might be too handsome for her. You just never know."

Before I can decide on a tack to destroy this "philosophy", an absolutely beautiful girl walks past and I say to Bangers, "Why don't you try your small-town luck with her. She's stunning."

"No way. You never go for a girl like that. She should be on telly. She could present the weather forecast. If she got her PHD in meteorology."

"What happened to that famous confidence?"

"It's not a matter of confidence. I might even get her, but you never want someone so far out of your league."

"What? Surely, you'd want to be with the best possible person you can be with?"

"And constantly feel like you're not good enough for them? And

155

worrying about losing them? I've been there. That way lies madness. It's a mistake you only make once."

"You could make it a few times." I reply quietly. Suddenly feeling as deflated as a ten-minute old carnival balloon, I gesture towards the approaching goth.

"Do you see this vampire woman coming towards us? I'm supposed to be going back to her crypt. Do you want me to introduce you to her and see how you guys get on instead?"

"You can't just swap me in if she likes you."

"Oh, she doesn't give a fuck about me."

"You don't fancy her?"

"It's not that. I'm still recovering from a sexy disease at the minute."

"Don't talk to me about diseases. Gonorrhoea? More like back-again-orrhea, haw? What's her name?"

"Let's not put labels on this."

"You *goth* it. Get it?

"You should definitely say that to her. Goths love puns."

"Do they?"

"No. Shut up"

"Is this turning into a group activity?" Fish Fingers says when she comes over. "We might need to pick up more lubricant."

"Actually", I say, "I think I'll just go home and write a poem denouncing the patriarchy. You should meet my friend though. I told him the safe word and explained everything. He understands completely."

"I don't know." she says appropriately unconvinced. I turn to Bangers, "Show her your tongue" He sticks it out like that second monster mouth in *Alien*. She's suitably impressed.

"You should get that thing pierced. I could do it for you." she suggests.

156

The Whistler

The next morning, me and Rooster are having breakfast in the kitchen while I read a book about apple tree pollination. I've got a plan to plant apple trees and all sorts of fruit bearers all over town. Turns out you need to plant two trees together to have sex for them to make apples. I find this botanical courtship very romantic. There's a Greek proverb in the book;

"A society grows great when old men plant trees whose shade they know they shall never sit in."

I'm not that altruistic or patient. It turns out you can produce raspberries and strawberries in less than a year. Life altering swan attacks aside, picking your own fruit is amazing. I'm thinking about what else I can plant in the park when the phone rings. Caller ID says it's Bangers.

"Hello?"

"Terro."

"What?"

"Thigh thin time in lub."

"Why are you talking like that?

"See pieced my tongue. See's samazin'."

I'll translate the rest, but just know it's taking Sherlockian levels of deductive reasoning to deduce what he's saying and he's spitting so much that my ear is getting wet down the phone line. I don't understand how this lizard man isn't choking to death if his tongue is swollen.

157

"It was the most sexually haunting night of my life."

"Oh God."

"I'm not one to kiss and tell bu-"

"But you're more than happy to bang and write a twenty-thousand-word thesis?"

"You know I've always considered myself an educator."

I hear the front door open, and Hotdog walks in.

"I'll have to call you back. The boy kissing machine has just gotten home." I hang up. I am absolutely not calling him back to finish that conversation. Hotdog slinks in covered in glitter and love-bites.

I bite my inner jaw, so I won't smile, "Well, well, fucking well. And where have you been? Rooster was worried sick."

Poor Hotdog looks too blissfully exhausted to play along.

"Right. Well, if you're gonna be embarking on this hedonistic voyage of sexual delinquency, Two Rules.

Rule One: No fucking glitter."

"What's Rule Two?"

"There is no Rule Two. How fucking hard can it be to follow one rule? Get in the shower and scrub that pixie jizz off you instantly before you infect the flat with a home décor disease that there's no cure for. We can't have you swanning about shedding glitter like a demented, whorish Tinkerbelle on crystal meth. We'll have to burn everything we own and you're already turning into a pyromaniac."

This doesn't even get a titter. He must be exhausted. He just smiles and heads for the bathroom. When he gets to the door, he turns to me,

"Mate?"

"Yes mate?"

"Thanks for coming with me last night. It means a lot."

I swallow the lump in my throat. "Don't get glitter on the bathmat."

Hotdog comes out of the bathroom whistling, wearing nothing but a towel, and puts some bread in the toaster. For a minute I'm too stunned to speak.

"What the fuck are you doing?"

"What? Making toast?"

"You're whistling. Shut the fuck up."

"I thought my happiness was important to you?"

"It's very important to me but so is your silence. Have you never heard the story of The Whistler and The Mechanic?"

"What? No."

"Allow me to enlighten you then, you ignorant slag! Once upon a time, years ago and miles away, quite recently, nearby, there was a mild-mannered mechanic who worked in a garage. You've never met a more even-tempered gentleman. He was a strict vegan and picked up litter on weekends. One day, a new mechanic came to work at the garage. He seemed a friendly sort. He was a hard grafter and got straight to work. The mechanic thought his new co-worker would fit right in. Until the new guy started to whistle. At first, the mechanic was puzzled at how oblivious the new guy seemed to be to how infuriating anyone with ears would find him as he vomited out this bile coated squealing. He whistled along with the songs on the radio. He whistled nonsense during the news and adverts. He whistled. Like a fucking bird. Like a feathery, flappy prick with a brain the size of a chickpea. He whistled and it was like a malevolent, deliberate snoring. It was verbal flatulence, tainting the universe. It was sonic pollution. It made the world ugly.

159

It began to strum a wicked string on the mechanic's soul that he never suspected was there. And for the first time in the jovial mechanic's life, he raised a hand in violence against his fellow man. This was something he would have previously thought impossible. He was punching the whistler in the face and when he fell, the mechanic fell upon him and he punched him in the face and he didn't stop and the blood was all over his own face and he licked his lips and it tasted salty and metallic and he punched him in the face until it wasn't a face anymore. It was just a head and he punched him until it wasn't a head any more, it was a puddle and still he punched and splashing about in it and the sound of his fist hitting the concrete was music to his ears and he still punched and he was screaming as his fist turned to pulp against the floor and his screams were music to his ears and he couldn't tell which were the shattered bones of his pulverised hand and which were fragments of the whistler's skull embedded in his flesh and still he punched this puddle that used to be a whistler and a puddle can't whistle and they found him like that and they were screaming as loud as he was and it was music to his ears because he knew they'd never whistle again after seeing what he'd done and the whistler's family would never whistle again and his hand was a stump and still he punched and splashed and screamed. As they dragged him away, he maniacally chanted 'I have another fist and a puddle can't whistle.' over and over again."

"Jesus Christ!" says Hotdog

"The whistler had only been there twelve minutes."

"What the actual fuck was that?"

"I know. Terrible, isn't it?"

"Did that really happen?"

"I wouldn't be at all surprised if it did. Did you hear the story about The Whistler and The Butcher? Once upon a time, years ago

160

and miles away, quite recently, nearby, there was a timid butcher, as gentle as a dove. He was a member of Amnesty International and a keen recycler. One day a new butch-"

"Alright! Jesus! I promise I'll never whistle ever again. Christ! Just shut the fuck up." he shouts as the toast pops.

"Great. There's some peanut butter in the top cupboard if you want some."

The Bloody Interweb

The next day, I'm in the middle of telling Hotdog a riveting story about a genial baker who beat his flatmate to death for buying supermarket brand ketchup when I notice that I don't have his full and rapt attention. The rude bastard is dicking about on his Interweb phone while I'm talking at him. He might need to hear the story about the candlestick maker who beat his mate to death for tapping about on a stupid lump of plastic while he was in company.

"What the hell are you doing on that new-fangled contraption?" If he's buying art by war criminals or Nazi gold, that thing's going in the freezer.

"I've found this online community of people who are in the situation I was in."

"There's a community on the Interweb? You stay clear of those people. I've met them. They're all maniacs who piss on the floor and eat puppies. Wait. What situation?"

"You know, when I thought God wouldn't accept me for being, you know, gay." He still whispers the word 'gay'.

Oh fuck! "Oh! Right. You haven't been telling people what happened, have you?"

"Of course, I have. There are people needlessly suffering because they don't know what I know. How could I not tell them?"

Fuckfuck! "I thought we decided we'd keep that between us?"

"I don't think we did. A lot of people are really interested in what I have to say. We're talking about meeting up. I thought I might invite them round here. You wouldn't mind, would you?"

Fuckfuckfuck! "Of course not. You're not gonna start a cult though, are you?"

"What? No. Don't be ridiculous."

"You're sure?"

"Yeah."

"That's a firm commitment then?"

"I promise you, I'm definitely not starting a cult."

"OK." I'm very worried.

Toggle Buttons

A few days later, I'm on my way home from the garden centre with a sack of apple tree seeds when I bump into Meatballs getting out of a van.

"There you are. My hero." he bellows on the verge of making a scene. He nearly rips my arm off shaking my hand.

"What's going on? Did you get a job or something?" I ask bewildered, gesturing to the van.

"Why would I do that? I've got my own business, don't I?"

"Those five dummies paid for that van?" I ask in a whisper.

"Of course not. With the money the first five brought in, I got a few more. Then I got creative just like you said. I'm basically Robin Hood. And that dog tip was gold."

"What dog tip?"

"Like you said, 'people don't care about people. People care about dogs.' I've got half a dozen stuffed dogs."

"Where did you get them?"

"I know a taxidermist."

"Where did you get the dogs though?"

"Never ask how the sausage is made."

"No!" I gasp.

"Jesus. I'm joking."

"About the whole thing?"

"Come on. I'll show you."

I'm led on a tour around town. It's like Madame Tussauds on crack. He's got dummies all over the place. They all move. He did something with levers, pulleys, and pistons. He tries to explain it, but I'm not listening. Basically, there are robots begging all over town. He's given them all back stories and set pieces. I've seen

163

nativity scenes with lower production value. There's a hippie with a guitar, but two of the strings are broken. He has a sign asking for money to fix it so he can busk again.

> I NEED STRINGS BUT THEY'RE NOT FREE
> WON'T YOU CHIP IN FOR SOME STRINGS FOR ME?

He's fucking dragged Pinocchio into this mess. Then we come upon one in old army camo trousers missing a leg.

"You faked a homeless, wounded army veteran?"

"Not unrealistic, I'm afraid. These heroes give everything they have to give for this country and then they're completely abandoned by the system and many end up homeless."

"Well, yea-"

"Suffering from PTSD and a range of mental health issues. Often turning to drugs."

"You cut his fucking leg off!"

"It's a metaphor."

We go a little further and I can't believe it. He's got one of those top of the line, realistic (but not really) sex dolls. She's Asian with pigtails dressed up like a university student. She's got a school bag and everything. Too far!

"I set her to vibrate, and people think she's sobbing. She's making me a fortune."

"This feels like we're getting suspiciously close to Sheriff of Nottingham territory here." but he's not listening.

"She's not even my biggest earner. Check this out."

We turn the corner and there's an elderly gent in a tweed duffel coat, shirt, and tie with a flat cap under his hood and a stuffed corgi sleeping/dead on his lap. It's tail wags from side to side like a wind shield wiper. His coat has those bloody toggle

164

buttons and everything. Despite knowing the whole scene is a sham, I'm heartbroken. Meatballs is a twisted artist.

"Don't you think this is a bit, I don't know, questionable? Morally?"

"What are you talking about? I'm stealing from the rich and giving to the poor. I'm basically Robin Hood."

"But you're not poor anymore."

"Yeah. It's working great. I'm gonna set some up in the next town over. You know, expand, just like you said."

"But there are real homeless people living there. Aren't you worried you'll be taking money people would have given to them?"

"Listen, in this world, you can either rip the piss or have the piss ripped out of you. Just like you said, fair is for fairy tales. I'm never playing by the rules again."

Oh fuck!

"The next step is to get a dozen more sex dolls like Ming-Lee over there and set up a robo-brothel."

Fuckfuck

"You're going to put Ming-Lee to work? But what about her educ- never mind."

"I'm being creative. This is all because of you."

"I wouldn't say that."

"No, seriously."

"No, seriously. Don't say that."

"You're far too modest but I do owe you big time. Your money will be no good in the robo-brothel."

"I don't think that's really my scene."

"Oh, don't worry. It's all very hygienic. All the robo-crotches are removable and dishwasher friendly.

"But what about the cups and plates?" I ask, horrified.

"What? Look, I've gotta see a man about a stuffed dog. I'll talk to you soon."

And he's off.

"FUCK!"

I run home to get Hotdog, but there's a weirdo convention taking place in the living room. You've never seen a more mismatched group of people congregated together in your life. They only seem to have one thing in common. They're hanging on Hotdog's every word. Apparently, he's a natural public speaker. He's using all these rhetorical flourishes. He's finishing sentences with "Why?" and starting the next one with "Because". Where the fuck is all this coming from? His audience are on the edges of my seats. I'd be scared if I could multitask. I head for the door, hesitate, go back for Rooster and leg it to Brie's. I bang on her door like a maniac.

"What's going on? You do realise you're the last man in Western civilisation to rock up to peoples' homes without calling ahead?"

"I'm in some strife with the old bill. I need your motor."

"Is there a reason you're talking like we're in a London gangster film?"

"Shut it Treacle. This is a bleemin' emergency."

"Look, I've had a long day, and I'm not really in the mood for your whirlpool of nonsense."

"This is my third Reasonable Favour."

"I'll get my keys. Why can't your bloody sidekick chauffeur you about?"

"He's busy. There's a herd of deplorables at our place."

"He's not having an orgy?"

"Worse. A séance. If you shaved the head of every crusty hippy currently chanting in my living room, you could make a filthy dreadlock rope to the moon."

"Why are there hippies in your flat?"

166

"A bunch of repressed, gay dudes are trying to get the green light from Jesus. I think we may be starting a cult."

"You really need to come clean about the Ouija board. This is getting out of hand."

"How can I? He's been kissing boys all over town. He'd never forgive me. Or himself. There'd be no convincing him he's not going to hell after all the rampant sinning he's been doing."

"I knew this would backfire."

"Congratulations." I say, exasperated.

"Why did you bring the rooster?"

"I was getting an animal sacrifice vibe. Can he lay low here?"

"You should really send him to live on a farm or something."

"I can't. He'd kill all the other animals."

"Where are we going?"

"I'll tell you in the motor."

"OK, this Cockney business isn't helping."

"I need your 'elp sweetheart."

"You listen to me, you mug. You call me sweetheart one more time and I'll carve you up like a Sunday roast at your mum's house. You got that, you slag?" she says doing an infinitely better impression than I've been doing.

"That was excellent."

"Thanks. I used to watch EastEnders. Now, what's going on?" We get in the car, and I explain the dummy scheme to Brie.

"With the missing leg? Beside the bridge?" She asks, "I gave that guy a quid and thanked him for his service."

"There's robots begging for change all over the place."

"And?"

"I need to get rid of the ones connected to the charity shop. My hippy boss knows I took them."

We drive around picking up the five mannequins I gave

167

Meatballs and I direct her to the bonfire site.

"You fed him your bullshit about basically being Robin Hood, didn't you?"

"A little bit, yes."

"You and Mystic Meg can't just keep flouting the conventions of civilised society while claiming to basically be Robin Hood. What on Earth made you think you were qualified to give anyone advice? On anything?"

"Everything I do, I do it for you."

At this point Brie looks at me like I've grown a second head.

"What? Erm . . . Wait! Are you quoting that bloody Bryan Adams song from the film?"

"It's a great pop song. Kevin Costner would be spinning in his grave if he knew what was going on."

"And if he was dead."

I light a fire and we throw the bodies on the pyre. As we watch the faces melt, Brie says "This is a tad macabre."

"A tad? It's dark as fuck."

"Do you really need to burn the video too?" I throw the tape into the flames.

"Kevin Costner gave us some terrible advice."

"Do you two do this a lot?"

"What? Clandestinely destroy evidence on the Badlands under the cloak of darkness? Just a bit."

"I wish you'd gotten him for this one too."

"Nonsense. You're doing fine. Besides, he's more of an insurance fraud kinda guy. He's not got the inner resources for dealing with the grittier elements of the underworld."

"And you have?"

"Some might say I've handled this with great aplumb."

"Gotham can rest easy tonight then. How many bystanders

do you think witnessed what appeared to be a man matching your description snatching homeless people all over town and throwing them in the boot of my car?"

"Oh balls! I need a drink. Let's go to a saloon."

We get to an inn and order drinks. The conversation comes back to Hotdog.

"I found tarot cards in the flat the other day." I tell Brie, "He got one of those phones that's linked to the information superhighway while he was at his parents' place and now, he's constantly on the bloody contraption talking to religious, gay people. We're definitely heading into cult territory."

"Don't you have to be charismatic to be a cult leader?"

"That's the thing. Since he's come out and stopped brooding, he's got the charisma of a serial killer. He' bloody magnetic. He even convinced me to let him whistle in the shower. If I'm not home."

"You need to tell him."

"I can't. He wouldn't believe me anyway and I can't exactly discover a second Ouija board under the floorboards. Who'd have ever thought that a good guy could take a slight ambiguity in the words of his god and go off the rails?

"You did geography in school instead of history, didn't you?"

"Yeah. Why?"

"No reason. I'm sure a vague notion about the formation of oxbow lakes and glaciation comes in handy just as much as all the events that led up to the way the world is today."

"What if he doesn't believe me? What if he does? He'll think I bamboozled him straight to Hell like when that snake convinced that girl that apples were delicious."

"Just be honest with him. Tell him what you did and that it came from a place of love. He'll be angry, but he'll forgive you."

"'A place of love'? Is it not enough that I love the fucker, I have to tell him as well?"

"You need to sort this out."

"You have been known to interfere with peoples' lives too you know." I point out.

"When?" she asks indignantly. I just raise an eyebrow at her.

"That was completely different." she protests.

The Dinner Party

Brie invited me to a dinner party once. It was a fucking nightmare. We have mutual friends but oddly, upon arrival, I didn't recognise a single soul there apart from the hostess. It was a strangely full house for a dinner party. Everyone seemed friendly enough, but their sandwiches were mostly pretty pretentious. I felt as out of place as a buzzard in a cuckoo clock. Luckily, I was wearing my cleanest shirt. I wasn't paying attention during introductions and having to call everyone mate, pal, or buddy made my conversation options pretty limited.

There was a fucking guy with a twisty moustache (Hummus & Halloumi) dressed like a train conductor from the start of the Industrial Revolution who all evening only put his portable phone down long enough to take his pocket watch out of his waistcoat to check the time. I thought records coming back was a bit pretentious, but it turns out that even time is better in analogue than digital now. I hate not being the worst person in a room. It always means there's some proper reprobates present.

Fourteen is a lot of mouths to feed, but Brie managed it. Dinner was good. We had some sort of African, tomato stew and it was actually a nice evening with only one major misstep on my part. A man who looked like Robert Smith from The Cure circa 1988 but with more guyliner (Venison) was talking about how he helped build an orphanage in Cameroon during his gap year. I zoned out and started wondering if a cow brought here from Cameroon and put in a field with local cows would have a different accent.

"Moo."

"Möôó."

". . . Moo?"

When I snapped out of it, a white girl with dreadlocks (Gorgonzola, Pear & Walnut) was talking about a recent trip to Malia.

"It was a huge mistake. So commercialised and overdeveloped. All I wanted was an authentic, cultural experience."

I was a bit taken aback to hear this from a hippy chick and chimed in, "Surely, improved infrastructure and development in such an impoverished and war-torn area can only be a good thing? Those people aren't there for poverty tourism." I opined with my most condescending tone.

They exchanged glances with each other, looking utterly baffled, and there was an awkward silence that went on for about two hundred years before Brie stuck her head around the corner from the kitchen. "*Mali* is a developing, war-torn country in central Africa. *Malia* is a tacky beach resort on the Greek island of Crete … Dickhead." Her look of glee was proportional to my mortification. And with that, her head disappeared back into the kitchen.

During dinner, I mostly managed to diffuse the tension I'd single-handedly conjured, and everything was fine. I listened to two girls (Spaghetti Shapes/Beans on Toast) discussing the carbon footprint of importing avocados from Mexico, "Like, it's just totally worth it." The frauds! When everyone was finished eating, the music suddenly cut off. Brie then made an extravagant stage entrance wearing a new mop head as a hat and a black sheet over her shoulders. She started tapping a fork on her wine glass until she had everyone's attention. In her most dramatic voice, she began,

172

"By now, you'll all be wondering why I've gathered you here tonight."

Nobody had been, but it's a strong opener. She held up her phone and pressed a button and the **DUN-DUN** sound effect from Law & Order bellowed from the wall speakers.

"You are about to enter my court. The people are real. The cases are real. The judgement is *final.*"

DUN-DUN

This elicited a bustle from the revellers. She continued, "ORDER IN THE COURT! A grave transgression has been ongoing, unchecked for years now. For far too long, this egregious delinquency has persisted unopposed. To quote the great Jean-Luc Picard 'The line must be drawn here. This far. No further.'"

"What crime are you talking about?" asked a girl, (Prosciutto/Mascarpone) with her head shaved, and a truly shocking array of clearly deliberately shit tattoos on display.

"Why, it's right before you and it's no mere peccadillo. It's a felony against fashion. I speak of course about you sir." Brie dramatically pointed at me.

"What?" I asked stupidly.

"Have you prepared an opening statement?"

"Are you joking?" I asked idiotically.

"If I was joking, you'd be laughing sir."

"What?"

"Very well. If you have no opening remarks, I shall begin. Ladies and gentlemen of the jury, you'll all be familiar with the expression 'Don't judge a book by its cover.' Brilliant literal literary advice. Banal, cliché platitude in life. Fashion can be a nebulous social construct I grant you, yet certain appurtenances are innately wrong and stir a primal repulsion in the hearts of man. I invite your scrutiny and scorn to Exhibit A, the defendants ridiculous visage."

173

"What?" I repeated even more dumbfounded, excruciatingly aware of all eyes being on me. Grown men should not blush, but I was radiating embarrassment and pinned to my chair by the weight of so much scrutiny.

"More specifically, I of course refer to the defendant's horrendous eyebrow piercing. This is a long, lugubrious tale of crimes against fashion ladies and gentlemen."

"Lugubrious?" I repeat, beyond lost at this point.

"Over the years, myriad endeavours have been fruitlessly made to cajole the defendant into seeing reason, yet he persists, intransigent. The scale of his poor judgement is truly Brobdingnagian."

"Brog-Ding-What?"

"It's from Gulliver's Travels, you dullard," she said. Then continued, "Alas, we have no recourse but to take litigious action and I fear we must be doggedly draconian in our ruling."

"Draconian?" Whatever was happening, it wasn't going in my favour.

"How do you plead sir?"

"What are you talking about? Who are all these people?" I ask looking around at this room full of strangers.

"Why, they are an impartial jury of twelve of your peers of course. Well, as impartial as anyone with eyes and intact eyebrows can be. Sir, it would behove you to treat these charges with the weight they deserve."

"Behove me?"

"I assure you this recalcitrant attitude will gain you no reprieve in this court. These proceedings are ineluctable. Now, how do you plead sir?"

"Not guilty? I reply uncertainly, "I've had this piercing for eight years."

174

"Yes. It was abhorrent the day you got it. It has been abhorrent every day since."

"Aren't I entitled to legal counsel?"

"You've demonstrated a myopic pathology of ignoring fashion council for years. You shall be defending yourself."

"This isn't fair."

"Fair is for fairy-tales sir."

"Objection?"

"Overruled." She bangs a previously unnoticed rolling pin on the table.

"Wait! You're the judge as well as the prosecution?"

"*Mater artium necessitas.*" she says lifting her head up in what can only be called a regal manner.

"What?" Was she speaking Greek?

"When needs must. I concede that it's highly irregular, but it was unavoidable."

"Why?"

"There's twelve jurors, you and me. I only have fourteen plates. You will restrict all further bellicose, rambunctious outbursts pertaining to my line of questioning, or you will be castigated with no dessert. Is that understood?"

"What's for dessert?"

"Banoffee pie."

"That's my favourite." I admit. She steps up right in front of me and looming over me like a cartoon villain, and triumphantly says, "I know."

"How are you doing this? You're making it impossible for me to understand you."

"Objection!" She bangs the rolling pin again. "Conjecture. You make a mockery of this court. I take great umbrage at the insinuation that I'm pontificating to discombobulate you by being

175

unnecessarily erudite or verbose. I assure you sir, that my diction is neither bombast nor bloviation. If you find my employment of appropriate nomenclature highfalutin, I'd suggest more fastidiousness in the future . . . Sustained. I'll caution the defendant to be less pugnacious."

"Can I have a dictionary then?"

"*Semper paratus.*"

"Huh?"

"No."

DUN-DUN

"Tell us in your own inane, simpleton words, what exactly you were thinking?"

"I got it when I was twenty-one. It has sentimental value. It symbolises my rebellion against conformity during my youth."

"Oh? Like a souvenir?" she asked in a mock reasonable tone.

"Exactly."

"That you keep on your face?"

"I think it looks good. OK?"

"I would agree with you sir, but then we'd both be wrong. The human visage is a tableau that requires no accoutrements."

"That girl has her nose pierced." I pointed at Prosciutto.

"Her name is Beating Drum and she's not on trial here." How had I forgotten that name? And how is it more ridiculous than her sandwich? That's one juror I'd already lost.

"Plus, *she* doesn't look like a Eurotrash drug dealer named Lars selling disco biscuits at a Scooter rave in Dresden in 1992. Let the record show that the defendant is as antagonistic as he is inarticulate."

"Objection."

"Ermmm . . . overruled."

DUN-DUN

"I would state for the record that the defendant is a friend of mine. His heroin-chic appearance is totally incongruous with his generally upstanding character. However, would you buy a slice of lasagne from this otherwise respectable, gregarious fellow? Would you loan him a hedge trimmer with confidence of its safe and timely return? Would you truly relax whilst on holiday assured in his assiduousness in feeding your pet turtle and putting your recycling out on Thursday night? I beseech you not to take pity on this fashion wretch. Your sole duty is to ascertain the answer to one simple question; does the defendant or does he not look like a cockwomble? Google claims that 'Punishment has five recognized purposes: deterrence, incapacitation, rehabilitation, retribution, and restitution.' We aren't here for retribution. We are here to rehabilitate. Some buffoons must be saved from themselves. A guilty verdict will be didactic, not punitive. Now, all in favour of getting rid of this abomination, raise your hands please."

Obviously, it was unanimous. They clearly hadn't forgiven me for the Mali/Malia debacle.

"How do you possibly intend to enforce this?" I ask.

"Sir, you are beholden to the court's indelible judgment. You will comply with its ruling."

"No. I won't."

"*Acta non verba.*"

"What does tha-"

She came at me like a rabid honey badger, twisted my piercing out and flung it out the open window like the last vestige of my youth. I was appropriately furious, but before I could say anything, she pulled twenty quid out of her pocket.

"You can buy a new one tomorrow."

"I'm too old to go into a shop and buy a new one." I admit.

"Ladies and gentlemen of the jury, the prosecution rests."

And with a flourish, she took a bow.

DUN-DUN

This received a rapturous round of applause. I was too
impressed to be genuinely angry, but I fumed for a few minutes for
forms sake. She'd earned it.

The hole in my eyebrow has healed since that night, but not
the one in my heart. Back in the now, she asks, "And how many
times have people tried to buy drugs from you since?"

"None." I admit, sadly rubbing my brow.

She looks around the tavern before saying, "OK, I'm gonna
head home. Are you ready?"

"For what? Oh! Fuck!"

"Look guilty. I'll see you soon."

"OK. Thanks for tonight." She winks at me, and her smile
turns into a mask of fury. I sigh in resignation and slouch in my
chair as she begins shouting at me for the whole pub to hear,

"That's the best you can come up with? She touched your
penis but not your heart? She's your first cousin, you sick fuck!"
And with that, she bolts for the door, leaving me to look like a
cousin fucker. She'll be furious when she gets home and realises
she has a feathery house guest spending the night who'll have her
up at dawn. It's important to savour the little victories.

Coming Out Out

The next morning, I wake up at bloody dawn anyway. I take what may be the most accurate piss of my life, go back to my room and do 500 sit-ups, 100 push-ups and 50 pull-ups. I'm making toast when I spot a book on the table that I've never seen or thrown at Rooster before. It's a compendium of all of Malcolm X's speeches. Is Hotdog learning how to orate? That fucker *is* starting a cult. He'd already gone to bed by the time I got home last night.

Later, I find him eating Rice Krispies out of an actual bowl. He looks contemplative.

"How did your meeting go?" I ask.

"Really good, I think. They all seemed really interested in what I had to say."

"Oh? You think you guys will get together again?"

"Absolutely. We're organising a function room at a pub somewhere. We'll need the space. A lot more people will be at the next meeting."

FUCK!

"Another thing." he says.

"Yeah? Go on."

"Let me tell you three good things first."

CHRIST!

- Puppies momentarily trapped under blankets.
- The feel of new socks.
- Hidden caves behind waterfalls."

179

"Those are good ones. What's wrong?"

He hesitates before saying "I'm thinking about coming out."

"I think that big gay ship has sailed pal."

"I mean to my parents." he says softly.

"Oh!" My jaw just about hits the floor. This is a terrible idea.

"What do you think?"

"Me? Erm, well. Do you think there's *any* chance they'll eventually accept it?"

"No."

"If there's not even a chance they'll come to terms with it, then maybe don't bother?"

"Just live a lie? I don't want to do that ever again."

"I hear you, but is not telling your parents stuff they'll never ask about living a lie? Especially sex life wise. Do you think I rang my mother when I started pissing lightning?"

"You being riddled and me being gay are hardly the same thing." he says, a little annoyed.

"No. Sorry. You're right."

"No. You're right. They'll never accept me while the church condemns me. The church is wrong though."

"I couldn't agree more mate."

"God said so."

"What? Oh! Yeah. I know, but what can you do? The Vatican isn't known for flip-flopping on major issues. You'd have to burn the whole Catholic Church to the ground and rebuild a new one in the ashes to change it." Was that a quote from something? I don't know. It sounds profound though. There's a thoughtful look on Hotdog's face. I can't say I like it.

The Grown Man Who Cried Wolf

A few days later, I'm passing through the town centre on my way to the library to see if rooster taming is a thing when I hear a big commotion. There's a crowd gathering in the street and pointing at the sky like there's been a Superman sighting. I look up and see a woman standing on the window ledge of the top floor of the county council building across the street. She's a jumper. She's got a baby in her arms. Oh God! I'm pretty sure those fireman bouncy castle things are only in American films, and the carnival isn't in town. It's windy, and the woman is shaking like crazy. All the shoppers and even the staff from the shops have come out to gawk. One hag (Corned Beef & Brown Sauce) shrieks with every gust of wind that rattles the troubled mother. I promptly suggest she dial it down.

As soon as the crone shuts up, I'm able to think clearly. Something's not right and I don't mean with modern society. It takes me a second to put my finger on it. Then, I realise what the problem is. I can't tell what type of sandwiches the woman likes. Is she insane? Is she a ghost? Have I got smallpox? Wait! Oh fuck! I turn around and look through the crowd. I spot him coming out of a jewelers. He has a ski mask on, but he'd need a lot more than that to hide from me. Meatballs!

"Fuck!"

I run to Brie's place as fast as my legs will carry me. I pound on her door. After what feels like a hundred years, she opens it.

"You really need to start making appointme-"

"Come on. We haven't got a moment to lose." There's a touch

181

of hysteria in my voice.

"Where are we going?" She sounds concerned.

"The pub."

We get to the closest speak easy that she hasn't humiliated me in, a trek that grows longer and longer all the time, and I get the double gins in and explain what I saw earlier without getting into the ins and outs of my swan issues.

"Wait! You just left her there? What if it was some poor, unhinged woman at her wits end?

"What do you mean I 'just left her there'? Did you want me to scale the bloody building like King Kong?"

"I was thinking more like Spiderman."

"Are you not listening?" I snap, "She wasn't shaking. She was vibrating. It was a Cabbage Patch Kid taped to a sex doll."

"OK, OK. I get it. Calm down"

I sag, defeated. "I've turned a nice hippy down on his luck into a crime lord. Is this all my fault?"

"What? Morally or like in a court of law?"

"Jesus! What should I do?"

"My only advice would be to wait five years."

"Yeah? Then what?" I ask hopefully.

"Nothing. This'll all just seem less of a huge deal in five years."

"Solid council."

"There's no point asking anyone else what they'd do. This wouldn't happen to anyone else."

"I have to do something."

"You could turn him in?" she suggests.

"How can I? Technically, this was all my idea. Plus, the police already think I'm a lunatic." I massage my temples, "And I never got a direct answer on what the story is with citizens' arrests."

"So, what then?"

"I have been on the lookout for a nemesis."

"You're gonna make him your nemesis?" Brie can be quite negative at times.

"I'd be lying if I said I wasn't considering making him my nemesis."

"You can't have a nemesis."

"I absolutely could have a nemesis. A lot of people who are a lot more reasonable than me have a nemesis."

"That's not true. Remember when you asked me what was the worst that could happen, and I was dubious? Well, even I would have never guessed you'd create a comic book villain, spark a cult of gay religious fundamentalists and plant enough food for the rat population to explode enough to reignite the black plague."

My stomach drops, "What?"

"Didn't you ever wonder why every tree in every park isn't a fruit bearing tree?"

"I did. That's why I did something about it."

"You're like a man with a fly swatter manically trying to swat a wasp while being completely oblivious to the fact that he's wandered into a theatre and stumbled upon a conductor's podium in front of an orchestra. You wanted to make some noise? It's music but it's shit. I've got my second reasonable request. Please don't ever attempt to intercede in my life like this."

"Are you sure? I did have a couple of ide-"

She cuts me off, "I'm bloody positive."

"How did it all go wrong? These fuckers are making a shambles of this whole philosophy I'm inventing."

"What? This whole notion about a fantasy world being founded on lies and deceit being better than reality?"

"I wouldn't put it like that."

"How would you put it?" I'm not prepared for this level of

scrutiny, so I go back to the bar and get more gins. When I get back, I quickly change the subject. "So, what's happening with you and Yo-Yo Guy? Things still up and down?"

"What's happening with you and that girl?"

"Which one?"

"What do you mean which one?" snaps Brie. She's suddenly gone from bemused to furious. "Which one do you fucking think? The fucking nice one who likes you. Not the fucking anti-Christ who dumped you *six* months ago."

"Why have you brought this up?" I say, taken aback.

"You started it with Yo-Yo Guy."

"Honestly, I just wanted to use that up and down pun." I'm sulking. I can't help it.

"You're not going to call her, are you?"

"She did give me an STI." I protest.

"The Banshee of Sodom gave you sexually transmitted frostbite. Then, she threw you out in the street."

"I did put her in the hospital." I whisper.

She rolls her eyes and puts a hand up, palm facing me in a halt gesture. "Just stop. You're hardly a woman trashing psychopath. It was a fucking accident. I'm sorry, but she'd clearly just been looking for an excuse to end it and that was it. She did it knowing full well how much you'd torture yourself over it, and she did it anyway."

I'm furious, "You haven't got a clue what you're talking about." I choke out.

"Let me tell you about the Yo-Yo Guy. I don't think it's gonna work out. He's obsessed with this idea of his ex. He's got this perfect idea of her in his head. A real person can't compete with an idea. Real people aren't perfect and he's beyond pedantic. Instead of finding a way to come to terms with himself, he's invested his self-worth in this horrible girl's opinion of him."

"Are we actually talking about Yo-Yo Guy?"

"Nah! I broke up with him last week. He was boring. Look, I'm sick of seeing you do this. You know, you really haven't changed a bit in the last twenty years. If you were half the glutton for banoffee pie that you are for punishment, I could roll you down the street. You still just want what you can't have. It's getting a bit fucking predictable darling. "

"That's not true. We lived together for a year and a half, and I was crazy about her."

"But did you ever really have her though?"

Oh fuck! I'm suddenly stunned and motionless like a squirrel in headlights. I'd give anything to go back to being furious.

"Look," she continues more gently, "I know you've had a tough time lately but there's a difference between having a broken heart and a bruised ego and it's past time you learned to tell the difference." She puts her hand over mine and pats it gently a couple of times before taking it away.

You know that bit between take off and the seat belt sign turning off when all the drinks you had in the airport bar hit your bladder like a ton of bricks and you're so desperate to piss that a blind panic sets in and you'd sooner rugby tackle that old lady before queuing behind her and you're suddenly furious at everything in your way? Well, I'm suddenly about to piss myself emotionally and I need to get the fuck out of here.

"Look, I need to go." I say standing up.

"I didn't mean to upset you."

"I know. It's OK." I've already got my coat on.

"But I haven't done my dramatic storm out?"

"I'll have to owe you one." And I'm out the door.

185

The Swan

It's dark when I leave the pub. I start towards home, but autopilot turns me into the park. None of the lights are working, but the moon is full. I start throwing stones in the pond like a petulant child throwing his toys out of his pram.

I was losing her. I'd always known I would. My nonsense started to annoy her, but it was my silliness that got her in the first place. My nonsense is involuntary. Knowing your favourite person is working up the nerve to leave you is a heavy burden to carry, and I couldn't even share it with her. Slightly more pathetic guys might snivel for reassurances, but you have to draw the line somewhere. I'd tried to spice up our sex life by making up my own racy positions. I came up with a vertical 69, but I didn't know my own strength.

Not Know Your Own Strength
The expression is only ever used by people who underestimate their own strength. It works just as well the other way.

There was a wrestler in the 90's called The Undertaker. Maybe there still is but I'm definitely too old to care. He had this famous wrestling move called The Tombstone where he would lift his opponents upside down with their face in his crotch and then drop them on their head ... She had to wear a neck brace for a month. I guess you could say I've become a tad obsessive about getting stronger since. I could give the undertaker a tombstone now. Or, you know, not. It's very important to have the option.

As soon as she'd cleared my name with the police, it was her turn to drop me. She said my sexual clumsiness was a health and

186

safety hazard. I'd always thought of it as *our* sexual clumsiness.

Since she'd left me, she'd stopped being a living, breathing, flawed person. She'd become a concept. She was the embodiment of sunshine and happiness. She was how I measured myself. If I could have made that Pesto Chick happy, I'd be a worthwhile human being. My own opinions of myself wouldn't matter. But half my notions and memories of her contradict the other half. In my head, she was tiny and petite while being able to reach a tin of peas on the top shelf. She was shy and demure and bold and confident. How could it all be true? Being ambushed by my emotions like this is making me nauseous. Women talk about these things, but men are supposed to swallow them. I'm about to try and swallow all of this like I always do but I'm afraid it will choke me.

Then, I see a fucking swan emerging over the blackness of the water, floating towards me, glowing white in the moonlight on a plane of darkness. Up until this point, I've crackled. I've even popped. Now, I snap. Overreacting *is* underrated. I start screaming at the swan as it approaches.

"Is it you? It could be you. You dickheads live for thirty years. I know. I checked. And that's only if you're not immortal. What the fuck do you want from me? What's with all the fucking sandwiches? What's the point? Am I supposed to be fighting crime? Are you magic? Are you like a rubbish, feathery, beady-eyed version of Aslan? Are you the reincarnation of my grandmother? Are you a metaphor for Catholic guilt? I really didn't think this story was that pretentious. I'm sorry. OK? I'm sorry I threw apples at you. I'm sorry I nearly robbed a bank. I'm sorry Hotdog started a cult. I'm sorry I created a Super villain and I'm very sorry that he paints homeless people in a negative light. I'm sorry I haven't bothered learning anyone's name in over twenty years. I'm sorry."

The swan opens its beak as if to speak and my heart stops, but all that comes out is a noise that sounds like the bloody Predator.

"Wait! You're not ... You're not just a fucking swan? Am I actually standing here under the moon, screaming at a normal dickhead swan? Christ! I've actually become a full-blown lunatic. No. If I had, it'd be a fucking relief. It wouldn't feel this embarrassing.

The Pesto Chick isn't a mercurial, Darwinian, inscrutable, tough love, independent, practical, unsentimental, apathetic, non-nostalgic, business and briskness, capricious, fiery, unsentimental, indifferent, particular, always worried about other peoples' opinions with a great memory, no nonsense siren. She's a horrible bitch! And I'm a fool.

Had I ever enjoyed her as much as I've missed her? I was thoroughly assessed, top to bottom, stem to stern. I was found lacking. I didn't get any constructive criticism at the end. When you eat a burrito or stay in a hotel, you leave feedback. I got nothing. I was just left to wallow and guess at my own shortcomings. Oh God! My heart wasn't fucking broken at all. I'd just had my confidence shattered. It crushed me. This is much more pathetic than I ever suspected. Revelations are horse shit. I nearly robbed a bank, for fuck's sake. I'm an idiot. Being properly, actually, self-aware for the first time in your life is a fucking nightmare when you're pathetic."

I appreciate that I could have had this revelation as an inner monologue, but screaming it at an innocent waterfowl who clearly thought I was throwing bread instead of stones really hammers the point home. When you're as thick as two planks, some points need hammering home.

I didn't overcome my intimacy issues at all, did I? I found a loophole. If you're with a horrible bastard who can't stand you, there really isn't any intimacy to have an issue with. But she is beautiful. There's no denying that. And I'm as shallow as a bowl of soup. I try to think of her superficial flaws. Her feet smelt like she took three years of ballet and two years of tap, dancing in cow shit. I'm not a scientist but I'm half convinced she grew so tall so her nose could get away from them. She has an outie belly button. I'd always thought they were just a disgusting myth until I saw hers. Instead of blowing, she'd whistle on her porridge to cool it in the morning. It drove me crazy. Is this helping? Not really.

There have been so many really nice girls who are now making nice guys really happy, but I wanted none of it. What could I have been thinking putting a bit of myself out in the world? I almost committed bananarmed robbery to get a girl's attention, I've instigated a cult of gay, religious fundamentalists and I'm the origin story of a maniacal criminal genius. Only I could be this divorced from reality and still be miserable. People as deluded as me are usually snug as bugs between padded walls thinking they're spies or Jesus or alien Elvis. I should be drooling and congratulating myself on saving the world, instead I convinced myself I'd managed to lose an angel.

Bored of the verbal abuse and doubtful any bread would be forthcoming, the swan splish splashes off into the darkness.

Bottom

My self-loathing levels are dangerously high the next day when I meet Hotdog by the fridge. He looks preoccupied.

"Alright?" I say.

"- Inscriptions in old books
- Christmas day mashed potatoes
- Clouds shaped like animals"

I sigh, and I'm about to tell him that I haven't got it in me, but I dig deep and say, "Go on. What's wrong?"

"I went to see the priest to talk to him about everything."

"Everything?"

"Me being gay, what God said and my new . . ."

"Followers?"

His brow furrows, "Friends."

"What did he say?"

"He said that the Ouija board was a fundamentally evil, spiritual practice and that the only way to God is through Jesus and that The Vatican condemns homosexuality."

Holy fucking Guacamole! Bastard!

"It might be time for another Reformation." Hotdog concludes.

"What does that mean?"

"You don't know what The Reformation is?"

"I could tell you all about volcanoes, stalactites and freeze thaw action." Even I can hear how ridiculous this sounds.

"We're planning a public protest for Sunday morning outside the church. There's gonna be placards and I'll be giving a speech. I've bought a high-tech, wireless speaker and everything.

190

It connects straight to my phone as a microphone."

"Remember when I asked you if you were starting a cult and you promised me you weren't starting a cult and I asked you if you were sure you weren't starting a cult and you said you definitely weren't starting a cult?

"Yeah?"

"I'm just making sure you remember."

"It's not a cult. I'm just not gonna have these people living in shame anymore. We're not gonna stand for it anymore."

Historians of the future will condemn me for not assassinating him now when there was still time. I'm really just too sad and defeated for this. Absolutely everything I touch turns to horse shit. I turn around and slink back to my room passing Rooster in the hallway. I close the door, get into bed and hide under the covers and wait for everything to be in the past.

Meatballs

Three days later, I go in Hotdog's room looking for some non-acidic socks. There's a notebook on his bedside table. On the cover, in his neat handwriting are three words *The Good Book*. He's writing a manifesto. I've created a monster. Actually, I've created two. I know these things are supposed to happen in threes but honestly, I'm up to my neck already. What was I thinking putting a bit of myself out in the world? I'm awful. What did I think would happen?

The next day, I'm plodding along on my way back from the supermarket, and as I'm passing the bus stop, I see Meatballs. I did have a whole speech prepared about how I'd thwart him at every turn and how I wouldn't rest until he was brought to justice, even though I'm still not sure what the story is with citizens' arrests, but I can't remember any of it now and I haven't got the energy. What the hell was my plan? To catch him using boobie traps and a big net? What the fuck was I thinking? He's actually a criminal mastermind with a master's degree in electrical engineering and I'm a daydreaming cockwomble. I'd probably just accidentally inspire him to start organ harvesting or something.

Before I can jump into traffic, he spots me and beckons me over. I'm lacking the inner fortitude to resist a beckoning today. I amble over. He has a massive backpack on his shoulders. The diabolical fucker could have anything in it. Before I can declare war on him or get a word in, the rude prick cuts me off.

"There you are now. I can't believe my luck. I'm so glad to see you. Honestly, I think it's fate meeting you here like this. There's something I need to tell you. I've done something kinda questionable. Morally."

"Yeah, and I'm going to sto-"

"I might have gone a bit too far, but I heard what you said

that first day and it really hit home. So, I did it. Just like you said."

"I nev-. Wait! Why are you at the bus stop? Where's the van?"

"I sold it. I sold everything. I'm on my way to the airport. I'm going to Mali to set up watering holes."

"What? You're going to Crete to set up a chain of bars?" The scoundrel!

"What? No. I'm going to Africa to dig wells. I stole from the rich and now I'm going to give to the poor. I've done some things that I'm not especially proud of though. The money may be dirty, but the water will be clean. None of this would have happened if you hadn't believed in me. I really hope you approve."

Mali is a developing, war-torn country in central Africa. Malia is a tacky beach resort on the Greek Island of Crete . . . Dickhead.

I'm utterly gob smacked.

"You. You're" I stutter. "You're actually Robin Hood."

"Yeah. Just like you said. Look, here's my bus. I gotta go. I'm really glad I got to see you before I left. Thanks for everything. You changed my life. You believed in me when no one else would even look at me."

And with that, he gives me a huge bear hug, chucks his bag in the luggage hold, and he's gone. I'm left standing there stunned and as the bus pulls away, I look down and notice my arm waving back and forth of its own accord, like one of his robots. This changes everything. Wait though. My nemesis. It isn't Meatballs at all. But if Meatballs isn't my nemesis. . . who else could it be except Hotdog? My oldest friend. The hero through misguided good intentions turns his best friend into a crazed cult leader corrupted by power and delusions of divine purpose. That'd be pretty poetic. For a dickhead who can't figure out a haiku. I need to stop him.

Snooping

Snooping is a soft, inoffensive verb for betraying someone's trust and violating their privacy. Rummaging, rooting and nosing are interchangeable yet slightly more unforgivable synonyms. Snooping just about sails in under the line as a frowned upon offense.

I'm snooping through Hotdog's room looking for insights into his dastardly machinations when I find *The Good Book* under his pillow. The zealot is sleeping with it. There's a pen stuck in the middle marking the page he's on. I brace myself for madness and open it at random. It's all in bullet points. I read the top one.

- When music is so loud, you can feel the bass in your chest
- Cracking the top layer of ice on a puddle with your toe
- The pronunciation of the word Demonstrable

I flick to another page.

- Climbing goats
- Fresh sheets
- Grass between your toes

I turn the page.

- Watching candy floss being made
- Water slides
- Kate Bush

It's a list. Of Good Things. There's pages upon pages of it.

The Fruity Harlot

I'm thinking about how to deal with Hotdog when there's a knock at the door. I freeze like a startled deer who has been startled. I consider hiding behind the sofa before I remember my newfound and very much forced and often resented lust for life. I steal myself and go to answer the door. Something as innocuous as answering your own front door shouldn't really require stealing but here we are. I take a quick moment to be unjustifiably proud of myself and I open this wooden portal on the unknown.

Oh God! It's Zesty. And she looks distraught.

"Strawberries!" she blurts.

"Sorry? What?"

"I need to talk to you."

"What's wrong?" As if I don't already know. This is it. This is fucking it. It's all over. This is it. This is fucking it. It's my own fault. I all but fucking dared the universe to turn my world upside-down. I'm going to be a father. This is it. My entire body goes into spasm. I'm nauseous, I've got goosebumps on my arms, the sweat on my back is prickly. This is fucking it. If I could breathe, I'd hyperventilate. I gesture her in and follow her into the kitchen.

Only I could sleep with someone once and catch chlamydia while getting her pregnant. Maybe she did it on purpose. To ensnare me. Pregnancy is the greatest snare of all. But who on Earth would want to ensnare me? I'm a fucking monster. Does everyone have completely reprehensible thoughts like this or is it just me? I guess there's no way to know.

There were so many things I never got around to doing before becoming a father. Like getting a vasectomy. I'll have to change nappies. I've not even come to terms with my own bodily functions

195

yet. I'll never sleep again. I was a great sleeper once upon a time. My personal space is a thing of the past. What if Rooster doesn't like the baby? Not being very likable isn't as effective a form of contraception as you'd think. Why isn't she on the pill? Mother fucker! Why am *I* not on the pill? There's a pill for men now. Because I didn't think it was healthy or natural to mess with my natural hormone balance so I decided that women should just keep doing it. How am I still this fucking selfish? Wasn't my character arc heading straight for redemption? I'm gonna turn this kid into a fucking serial killer, I just know it.

I need to take a shower. I'm not crying in front of this stranger. No! It's important I make a good showing of myself here. I won't ask if it's mine. She wouldn't be here if it wasn't mine. I'll be concerned for her with a tinge of pleased. That'll be good. She'll appreciate that. That'll be the thing she remembers. Here it comes. This is fucking it. I might be sick.

"This is hard to say." It's hard to hear. "Remember when you put the rice in the curry?"

Unbelievable!

"I think you did it again. I think you might have poisoned me or something."

She's not pregnant. I just poisoned her. She's talking and clearly distressed but I'm so relieved I haven't heard a word. Focus dickhead!

"Say all that again." I say.

"Where did you get that mad meat from? Was some of it actually exotic? I think there might have been something wrong with it."

"The meat?" I ask, baffled, "What are you talking about? It was fine."

"Did I really eat a giraffe?"

"What? Are you sick?"

"I think" she hesitates. There's tears in her eyes now.

"I think I'm going crazy."

"What?"

"Ever since the Mega Tropical Barb-"

"Turbo Exotic Barbecue" Why the fuck am I correcting her? Shut up dickhead!

"My mind has been playing tricks on me."

"What kind of tricks?"

"It must be the meat. Maybe it had some weird tropical disease in it. I mean, who the fuck eats giraffe?" I feel such a pang of guilt that it actually makes me flinch.

"There was nothing wrong or exotic about the meat. I promise." I stress. "What kind of tricks?"

"What else could it be? I don't want to go crazy. My auntie went crazy. She's locked up in a mental asylum now. She thinks it's 1986, and she's one of the girls in Wham. She keeps saying she wants to dance with George, not Andrew. I don't want that to happen to me." Tears are running down her face. What the fuck is she talking about? I put the kettle on. It might be the only thing men are good for in these situations. Then I take her hand and I try again. "What kind of tricks is your mind playing on you?"

"I'm hallucinating. I keep having these flashes. When I see people. Everyone."

Oh no!

"What happens *exactly*?" I press.

"It's so strange. Everyone I see, I see a fruit in front of them for a second. I might be becoming obsessive compulsive or something. I've been working on that bloody market way too long. I have a degree in history for God's sake. It started the day after The Turbo Exotic Barbecue."

Oh fuck!

"You're not hallucinating, and you're not obsessive compulsive. And if you have a disease, it's not tropical."

"What? How do you know?"

"Come on. I'll show you." I put on my jacket and grab a bingo clipboard left by a previous tenant that we've never found any use for and a random high vis vest.

"What are those for?"

"With a high vis vest and a clip board, you could walk into Buckingham Palace or the Oval Office or a bank vaul-" I shake my head and sigh. You could walk into a bank vault. Not now! I lead Zesty around the corner to the main street.

"Where are we going?"

"Just here. Stand right there." We stand outside the corner shop, and I hold up the clipboard like I'm reading from it. I stop the first person to come along.

"Excuse me sir. Can I ask you one quick question for a survey?"

"Sorry. I'm in a rush."

"We're not interested in your bank account information or your immortal soul." I reassure him. He comes to a sudden halt.

"Oh! Go on then."

"We'd just like to ask you what your favourite fruit is?"

"Oh? OK. Errm. Peaches."

"Thank you for your time."

"Is that it?" he asks suddenly suspicious.

"Yeah."

"But you haven't written it down."

"Move along sir."

I repeat this another dozen times before turning to Zesty.

"Did you get even one of those wrong?"

"Just one."

"Really? Which one?"

"You."

"Me? What do you mean?"

"When I look at you, I see a strawberry, but you're obsessed with bananas."

"I'm really not. Strawberries *are* my favourite. You're not crazy."

"How do you know all of this?"

I look up the street and see a very pregnant woman in dungarees waddling towards us.

"Tuna, ham, pickles and potato salad" I whisper to Zesty.

"What?"

"Excuse me" I say to the lady waving the clipboard "Super quick. Could you tell us your favourite type of sandwich please?"

"OK." She slowly says in confusion. "It's strange but ever since I've been pregnant, I can't get enough of tuna, ham and potato salad all together with pickles on top."

"Thank you very much." She shrugs, smiles and waddles on her way.

"What the hell is going on?" asks Zesty all moon eyed. "How long have you been able to do this?"

"You heard about the time I got attacked by that swan? Out of nowhere? Completely unprovoked?"

"Yeah?"

"Yeah."

"The swan did it?"

"If the nuns didn't know voodoo."

"What other powers do you have?"

"Powers?"

"What else can you do?"

"Absolutely nothing."

"Wait! So, I caught this from you?" she accuses. "Did you know this would happen?"

"Absolutely not. This has never happened before."

"Well, how many girls have you slept with?"

"Oh, I don't think that's any of your business."

"Then, why me?"

"Well," I say sheepishly. "It wasn't exactly a one-way street."

"What exactly does that mean?" she demands. I really hadn't planned on doing this.

"I kinda got something from you too. Chlamydia." I'm ready for her to be furious or to deny it, but she just bursts into tears in the street.

"I'm so sorry. My ex denied it, but I knew he was fucking around. This is so humiliating."

Fuck!

"Hey. It's not your fault. These things happen."

"I suppose." she says, sniffling and drying her eyes with her sleeve. "How do I get rid of it?"

"You just take some antibiotics, and it goes away in a week."

"The fruit thing will go away?"

"Oh! I meant, you know, the Chlamydia. The other thing you're stuck with I'm afraid. I'm sorry."

"I can't get rid of it?"

"I never have." I say as gently as I can.

"I'm stuck like this forever?" she slouches, "Seeing fruit every time I look at someone?"

"It could be a lot worse."

"How exactly?" And she's pissed off again.

"Other things can effect it. I had a man flu once and I could tell if people had washed their hands or not after they'd last been to the bathroom. Absolutely no one had."

"That's disgusting."

"I once had tonsillitis and I could tell what everyone's favourite soup was."

"What was that like?"

"Everyone just likes Leek & Potato."

"Oh."

"I had shingles when I was seventeen and for two weeks, I saw everyone in their underpants."

"Ha! Really?" This seems to have cheered her up. "You must have loved that when you were seventeen?"

"Being an involuntarily peeping Tom? There's nothing nice about seeing people with no clothes on if they don't want you to. And are you aware of how many truly elderly people live in this town? I am."

"So, when you get sick, your powers change?"

"Powers? Calm down Boy Wonder."

"You don't know though. If you caught myxomatosis or rabies, you might be able to move things with your mind or hypnotise people or fight crime or something."

"Have you ever seen a man when he's sick? I'd be too busy having Myxomatosis and complaining to do any of those things."

"Do you wanna grab a drink? I've got a million questions to ask you."

"I can't. I've actually got a lot on."

"Oh!" She looks hurt. And I *have* infected her brain.

"You could come along if you like? I could use the help."

"Yeah?" she asks hopefully.

"Did you come in your car?"

"Yeah."

"Does it have a full-size boot?"

She looks slightly worried, "Yeah?"

"Great. We'll need it."

"Wait. What are we doing?"

"It's a long story."

"How long?"

"We're approaching novel length."

Bush

Hotdog takes the same shortcut down the lane and across the back field behind our flat on his way home every evening when the weather's good. Today, he walks down the lane and turns the corner and sees a burning bush. He stops in his tracks, looking around confused. Then, the bush speaks to him in a light and friendly, feminine voice.

"Hello there"

"God?"

"Yes. It's me. Hello."

"You're a woman?"

"Yes, I'm a woman. Don't be bloody sexist." God sounds snippy.

"Oh! Yeah. S-sorry. I'm v-very s-sorry." he stutters.

"Calm down. It's fine. I believe you've been looking for me."

"Yes God. I've been spreading your good word, about you know, you being cool with the gays. People don't believe me mostly."

"That message was just for you. People need to find self-acceptance in their own way."

His eyebrows furrow, "What? Why though? A lot of people are suffering like I was. It seems needless. You could clear it all up in a second?"

Zesty covers the microphone with her hand and whispers to me, "What the hell do I say to that?"

"I don't know. I didn't think he'd pick today to suddenly wonder why there's suffering in the world."

"I need to tell him something?"

"Trust yourself." I tell her. She uncovers the microphone on her phone.

"I move in mysterious ways. People take different roads on

203

their journeys to inner peace."

"That's good." I whisper.

"Thanks. I saw it on a meme."

"What's a meme? Wrap it up before the speaker melts or we burn the whole field down."

"Lay off with the séances and psychic nonsense and stop spreading my word. I'll take care of that myself. Don't come looking for me. If we need to talk, I'll come to you, got it? Stop trying to hog miracles and disband your cult."

"It's not really a cult God. It's jus-"

"*Disband your cult!*" God booms.

"Yes God."

"Good, now get your-"

"God?" he interrupts.

"Yes?" God sounds impatient.

"Can I ask you a favour?"

"I don't really do favours."

"It's not for me."

"Go on then."

"It's my best friend. He's been very good about me being gay and well, everything really. He's very unhappy God. I think he hates himself. Is there any chance you could help him make peace with himself the way you helped me?"

Zesty looks at me like I'm an injured puppy.

"The speaker." I snap at her.

"Oh!"

"I'll see what I can do. Now get yourself home as fast as you can and . . . say three Hail Marys."

"Yes God. Thank you God." And with that, Hotdog takes off at a sprint. As soon as he's out of sight, I run out with the fire extinguisher and put the bush out.

"I've told that fucker repeatedly that I don't want him praying for me." I pick up the speaker and inspect it. "It's all melted." I turn to Zesty, "You were absolutely brilliant though."

"Thanks." she says looking shy but pleased.

We dig up the burnt bush and replace it with a miraculously unburnt one. We got two for twenty quid at the garden centre. We take the singed one and what's left of the speaker to the bonfire sight and burn them to cinders.

Standing side by side watching the flames, Zesty asks, "Do you do this kind of thing often?"

"No. Well, actually yeah," I say with a goofy smile plastered across my face. "I suppose I do."

"You're a good team, you two."

"You think so?"

"Yeah, you've gone to all this trouble for him."

"To be fair, it was my fault he was about to turn into Jim Jones. And I destroyed his new speaker." She ignores this deflection and continues.

"And he'd have used his one wish in the world to make you happy." This sudden and emotional deluge of sincerity briefly makes my skin crawl, but I'm OK.

"Would you like to grab a drink?" I ask.

"Yes!"

She picks a slinky cocktail bar, all chrome and recessed lighting. Zesty is fascinated with her sixth sense, so we sit by the window and people watch while we talk.

"See that guy?" she says.

"Yeah?"

"Grapefruit."

"Fucking grapefruit? You know what else?"

"What?"

"Easy single plastic cheese on white bread."

"What?" she laughs, "The boring bastard."

"I can't prove it at the moment, but I bet he doesn't wash his hands either."

She laughs again. I find myself having a very nice time.

"This is fun." she says.

"Yeah, it is. It isn't usually."

"Maybe you just needed someone to share it with." I look at her dubiously, but she continues.

"I just kinda wish mine wasn't fruit. I really get enough of that at work."

"You know, I don't think it is."

She raises an eyebrow, "What do you mean?"

"It's fruit when you have Chlamydia. You'll go to the doctor tomorrow, get antibiotics and in seven days, who knows what it'll be. You might shoot lasers from your eyes." She perks up as this idea develops in her head.

"Or flowers might burst into bloom whenever I walk past."

"Yeah, mayb-"

"Or I might be a muse, and everyone will become incredibly creative whenever I'm near."

This girl is a whimsical lunatic.

She goes on, "You know what this means, don't you?"

"What?"

"Magic. It's real." There's an honest to God look of wonder on her face.

"It's just sandwiches and fruit." I say unconvinced.

"That doesn't matter. This could be the tip of the iceberg. And even if it's not, it still doesn't matter. It still means that there's definitely magic in the world. That's amazing. That's enough. A little bit of magic can go a long way."

"I never once thought of it that way." I really am an idiot.

"Of course, you didn't. You need someone to point out the positives in front of your face. WB Yates said that 'The world is full of magic things, patiently waiting for our senses to grow sharper'."

I sit bolt upright as this, "Jesus! Did he?"

"He did. I wasn't going to see you again, was I?"

I slouch back in my seat and sheepishly ask, "What makes you say that?"

"You had vitamins on the kitchen table. Only someone who has no intention of eating any fruit or veg needs vitamins." This girl is much smarter than me.

"It's not you." I start.

"Oh, I know that dickhead." she says with a smile.

"To be honest, you're probably better off."

"Prawns!" she exclaims.

"What?"

"Prawns! Prawns were the only thing at your Turbo Exotic Barbecue that weren't Turbo Exotic. You knew, didn't you? That I like them? You got them just for me?"

"Em, I guess I did."

"I think you're pretty nice deep down." This poor girl has clearly been treated terribly in the past.

"You know," I say, "I should probably check in on you in seven days when you're cured. Just to check what you can do. You know, just to make sure you can't turn people into stone and the power doesn't corrupt you. I wouldn't want you to turn into my nemesis."

"You have a nemesis?"

"I must have one out there somewhere. Surely."

"So, it's a date then."

207

"I don't know if I'd sa-"

She speaks over me, "It *is* a date then. I'll pick you up from your place. In seven days.

"Should we swap numbers? Just in case something comes up."

"You mean an escape clause? No. You won't be needing one of those." She gets up to leave.

"What time?" I ask.

"Sundown." And before I can ruin everything, she leans over, kisses me on the cheek and whisks away. Wow! It's not often you get to see a girl properly whisk away.

Hotdog

I get home to find Hotdog sitting at the kitchen table waiting for me.

"How was your day? Get up to much?" I ask him pointedly.

"Nope." He pops the P. He's a terrible liar. "I have decided to disband my . . ."

"Cult?" I suggest.

"It wasn't a ... yeah." he says, lowering his eyes in shame for a second.

"That's good." I say lightly, taking off my coat.

"How about you?" he asks, "How are you doing?" He's observing me closely. It takes me a second to realise what he's looking for, but I put on a big smile for him.

"I feel . . ."

"Peaceful?" he suggests.

"Yeah. Peaceful. How did you know?"

"Just a lucky guess." he says all coy and smug. He's looking at me like I'm a healed leper. The adorable idiot. With a friend like this, who needs a nemesis? My smile doesn't need much help just now. And then, I have it. The big revelation. Meatballs! If my nemesis isn't Meatballs. And it isn't Hotdog. Bless him. There's only one person left it could be. Zesty! No. Not really. It's me. I'm the villain in this story. But I'm the hero too. I'm winning, but only at defeating myself. I'm my own nemesis.

I think back to Blackberry Jam. Old people have always made me feel incredibly sad but getting old isn't a tragedy, not if you've really lived. The only tragedy in that hospital room that day was me and Hotdog ... Maybe the guy with the eye-patch too. We really should have looked further into what was going on with him. Those two blackberry jam lovers had lived full, sexual lives. Me and

Hotdog hadn't lived at all. Time passing isn't sad, and it doesn't need to slow down. It only needs to be made the most of.

"Mate? asks Hotdog.

"Yes mate?"

"What are you gonna do?"

"Me? What I told the priest I'd do. Write the book."

"With the blood, sweat and tears?"

"And the sperm." I agree, "On every single page."

"You're gonna need a lot of sperm."

"Yep!"

"I hope anyone reading it is wearing gloves." He says, unforgivably breaking the forth wall.

"I really hope they are too." I agree.

So, what have we learned? Is Zesty the one? No. It's all this nonsense about The One that got me in trouble in the first place. This isn't The Matrix. Will it go anywhere? Of course not. This is a character arc, not a character razor. It's not supposed to be sharp enough to cut yourself on.

She's not perfect. I know that going in. She snores, she's basically riddled, and her superpower is even more boring than mine. She's not too good for me. Feeling like you're not good enough for someone isn't a good thing. Zesty hasn't lit a fire inside me, but who in their right mind would want to be on fire? That's a mistake you only make a dozen times, but is being with her better than being by myself? It's much better. She's much better company than I am. She does have Chlamydia, but due to the miracles of modern medicine, it'll be gone in a few days. She isn't a model or an astronaut. I think I'm OK with that though. She does have one miracle attributable to her already, and she did bake me a loaf of disgusting banana bread. A little bit of magic does go a long way.

I'm excited for our date but it's just a bonus. That gnawing feeling in my stomach is gone. Not because I've accomplished anything. It doesn't really matter if you become an astronaut or not. Honestly, it can be pretty lonely down here. I'd be miserable on the moon. It doesn't matter if you accomplish nothing more than planning a bank robbery, faking a miracle, playing a tiny part in the origin story of a modern-day Robin Hood or giving a girl psychic rabies and then planning a hot date with her. You might just tell the story of the time you put rice in a curry over a decade ago in the most elaborate fashion possible. It only matters that you're making the most of it.

At the end of the day, if I'm not actually Robin Hood, that's my only job, spending my time, instead of trying to save it. If you go outside, anything could happen, honestly. This isn't the daunting prospect it used to be. This is my life, I guess. I don't feel like I'm wasting it. I think it's pretty charming actually. Plus, I have a lot on. As well as making sure Zesty's "powers" don't corrupt her, I've got a list of stuff to bury on the beach for Beetroot to find and I need to introduce dozens of hawks to this town to kill the plague of rats who are about to arrive to eat the bounty I've planted.

"Fancy a bonfire?" I ask my friend.
"Yeah, OK. What are we burning?"
"Time pal. Just time."
"Cool. Oh! Mate? Hotdog asks.
"Yes mate?"
"Have you seen my new speaker? I can't find it."
"No mate."

Every man writes his own moral code. Some of us do it in crayon.

Printed in Great Britain
by Amazon